RETURN TO BELLA TERRA

A NOVEL

BY

MARYANN DIORIO

BOOK 3 OF *THE ITALIAN CHRONICLES TRILOGY*

TopNotch Press
A Division of MaryAnn Diorio Books
Merchantville, NJ 08109

RETURN TO BELLA TERRA
by MaryAnn Diorio

Volume 3 of *The Italian Chronicles* Trilogy

Published by TopNotch Press

A Division of MaryAnn Diorio Books

PO Box 1185 Merchantville, NJ 08109

Publisher's Note: This is a work of fiction. Names, characters, places, and incidents either are the product of the author's imagination or are used fictitiously. Any resemblance to actual persons living or dead, business establishments, events, or locales is entirely coincidental.

Copyright 2017 by MaryAnn Diorio

Some Scripture quotations are from the ESV Bible (The Holy Bible, English Standard Version'), Copyright © 2001 by Crossway, a publishing ministry of Good News Publishers. Used by permission. All rights reserved.

Some Scripture quotations are taken from the Holy Bible, New Living Translation, Copyright ©1996, 2004, 2007, 2013, 2015 by Tyndale House Foundation. Used by permission of Tyndale House Publishers, Inc., Carol Stream, Illinois 60188. All rights reserved.

Softcover Edition: ISBN: 978-0-930037-24-6

Electronic Edition: ISBN: 978-0-930037-38-3

Library of Congress Control Number: 2017913113

While the author has made every effort to provide accurate telephone numbers and Internet addresses at the time of publication, neither the publisher nor the author assumes any responsibility for errors or for changes that occur after publication. Further, the publisher and author do not have any control over and do not assume any responsibility for author or third-party websites or their content.

Cover Design by Lisa Vento Hainline.

Praise for the Fiction of MaryAnn Diorio

The Madonna of Pisano

"From the first couple of pages my emotions were pushed into chaos. I kept wondering at how easy it is for people to believe a lie and allow doctrine to be their truth …. This is one beautiful story that makes Christ the Redeemer shine so brightly."

~ Amazon Customer

"Excellent characters, dramatic plot. Beautifully written, giving wonderful feeling for the setting in place and time. Emotionally intense situations, satisfying resolution. Among the two or three best novels I have read this year. Highly recommended."

~ Dr. Donn Taylor, Novelist and Former Professor of Literature

A Sicilian Farewell

"Such lovely writing—and an even lovelier story! Author MaryAnn Diorio takes her readers on a courageous journey, from the ancient romance of the Old Country to the perils and possibilities of the New Country. Well-developed characters and a story that will stay with you long after you've finished this enjoyable read."

~ Kathi Macias, Award-winning Author

Surrender to Love

"I enjoyed reading *Surrender to Love* by MaryAnn Diorio. It was a short story that packed a powerful punch. Anyone who has ever experienced loss in their life, in any form, can automatically relate to the feelings of Teresa and Marcos in this book. In addition, there were three characters, each of whom experienced significant loss—but each from a different perspective; this brings even more depth to the book. It showcases how, despite knowing "what to do," it's not always easy to tell your heart to do what your head knows it should. And that saying goodbye can feel like a betrayal of sorts…letting go of the old is more than just head knowledge—it has to come from the heart, a full surrender."

~ Cheri Swalwell, Book Fun Magazine

A Christmas Homecoming

Winner of the Silver Medal for E-Book Fiction in the 2015 Illumination Book Awards Contest sponsored by the Jenkins Group.

"This short story is a wonderful way to start the Christmas season. It is a story full of human emotion and the struggles this life can challenge us with. The lesson throughout the story is that all things are possible through God's grace. This is a 'feel good' story that lifts the spirits and keeps you encouraging the main character to persevere and not give up. It is a great book for a short respite from our busy lives."

~ Kimberly T. Ferland, Amazon.com

"Well-woven. If only all stories made me sit on the edge of my seat, unsure of the outcome, but desperate for a good conclusion for the characters!"

~ Sarah E. Johnson, Poet

"A great Christian read. A powerful short story packed full of love, hope, heartbreak and a strong message on forgiveness."

~ Jerron, Amazon.com

ACKNOWLEDGMENTS

Books are the fruit of the efforts of far more people than simply the author. Books are born from the combined efforts of many people with multiple talents, all of whom pool their resources to produce a work that is worthy of its readers. Such, I trust, is the case with this novel you are holding in your hands.

Above all, I would like to thank God my Father in Heaven for giving me the idea for this book. He is the Giver of every good gift. This story is a gift from His heart to mine. Thank You, Father, for entrusting me with Your gift. I worship You!

I would like to thank my Lord and Savior, Jesus Christ, for sustaining me as I wrote this book. Lord Jesus, You are the Awesome Redeemer, the One Who makes all things new. Thank You for renewing me as I wrote this story of Your heart. I love You!

I would like to thank You, Holy Spirit, my precious Guide and Counselor, as You unfolded to me this story of Your heart. I could feel Your Presence hovering over me as I wrote. Thank You for guiding me on this creative journey and pointing me in the direction of Your choosing. I adore You!

Heartfelt thanks are also due to my superstar husband Dominic who did much of the historical research that serves as the background for this novel and who did the grocery shopping, the cooking, and the cleaning as I worked tirelessly "in the zone."

Deeply, deeply loving thanks to my precious daughters, Lia Diorio Gerken and Gina Diorio, who prayed me through the tough times. I am so honored to be your Mom. You are the best!

Deep, deep thanks go to my awesome Prayer Team—Dr. Adeola Akinola, Sandra Marrongelli, and Devata White—who stood beside me every step of the way, upholding me through the many trials that presented themselves during the writing of this book. Love and blessings to you!

A very special thanks to my editor, Mr. Frank Kresen, whose insightful comments made this story so much stronger because of his editorial skills. Thanks also to my first readers, my husband Dom and daughter Gina, who gave me valuable insights regarding plot.

Last, but certainly not least, sincere thanks to my precious readers. Without you, this book would have no home. May its home be your heart. May it bless you and touch the deepest places within you with the redemptive and healing love of Jesus Christ!

DEDICATION

To my Amazing Husband ...

Dominic Diorio

You are my best friend and my hero!

~ ~ ~

To my Precious Daughters ...

Lia Diorio Gerken

and

Gina Diorio

You are the jewels in my crown!

~ ~ ~

Above all,

To my Lord and Savior Jesus Christ ...

You are my very Life!

RETURN TO BELLA TERRA

"Anyone who wants to be my disciple must follow me."

~ John 12: 26 NLT

Return to Bella Terra

By

MaryAnn Diorio

Chapter One

"Dear Maria, you must come quickly! Mama is dying!"

Maria Landro Tonetta's heart lurched. She grabbed the edge of the kitchen table as she read the telegram from her younger sister Cristina. It was dated two days before. What if Mama had already died?

With trembling hand and tear-filled eyes, Maria continued reading. "Mama wants very much to see you again before she dies. Can you come right away?"

Of course, she could. Not only could she, but she must. Her heart raced. She would book passage on the next ship that sailed to Sicily, provided there was still room. Ships sailed from New York to Palermo approximately every two weeks, and manifests filled up quickly.

Outside the balcony door window, the only window in the tiny tenement house flat, a steady snow fell thick and fast. January had begun with a fury.

And so had Maria's day.

Her throat tightened. Would she ever see Mama again?

Guilt washed over her. When she'd left Sicily eight years earlier, she'd promised Mama she would come back for a visit. A promise never kept. Not for lack of desire, but for lack of money.

A lump formed in Maria's throat.

No one had told her and Luca that life in America would be difficult. Discouraging. At times, deeply depressing. The claims of streets of gold had proven false. Instead, they'd discovered streets of tin. The claims of beautiful homes had

1

turned into crowded, roach-infested tenement houses that often bred violence as well as disease.

And the claims of well-paying jobs had turned into long hours of hard labor that barely allowed them to make ends meet.

Worst of all, no one had warned them of the deeply felt hatred and prejudice against Italians, particularly Italians from Sicily. No one had warned them of the condescending ethnic slurs, the continual threats on their lives, the horrendous assaults, and the vicious discrimination in the workplace, particularly against Italian women. No one had warned them of a brutal life that, so often, had made her want to return to Sicily and to *Bella Terra*, the beautiful hillside farm where she'd grown up.

And the home where Mama now lay dying.

Hot tears spilled from Maria's eyes onto the telegram, blurring the words. She must leave immediately. It would take more than two weeks, if not longer, to cross the Atlantic Ocean back to Sicily, especially in winter. She had no time to spare.

But what to do first? Her husband, Luca, would not be home from his job on the railroad for one more day. He'd been forced to take the position laying rail for a new stretch of the Pennsylvania Railroad shortly after his release from prison. Should she wait for him to return before booking passage on the next ship? If she did, she would run the risk of delaying their arrival in Sicily by an additional two weeks.

And what if Luca wanted to go with her? She shook her head and sighed. That was out of the question. Their finances barely permitted one round-trip ticket—let alone two. Besides, who would care for Anna and Valeria? She could ask Enza Addevico, her good friend and neighbor who lived in the apartment down the hall. But leaving her children with Enza for an extended period of time would be a terrible imposition, not to mention Maria would miss them terribly.

But miss them she must. She took a deep breath. No. She would have to go to Sicily alone. There was no other way. Her greatest regret was that Mama would not see her grandchildren one last time before she died.

The thought of traveling across the Atlantic Ocean alone filled Maria with dread. The voyage from Sicily to America eight years earlier had been a nightmare. But at least she'd traveled with her husband and children. Traveling alone would mean she'd have no protection.

Except Mine.

The Lord's gentle reminder triggered a twinge of guilt. "Of course, Lord. Please forgive me." She whispered the confession under her breath and received His forgiveness.

She folded the telegram and placed it in her apron pocket. If only a thought could transport her to Mama's side! How Maria missed her! How she regretted not once visiting her since leaving Sicily!

Her heart clenched. *God, please keep Mama alive until I get there.*

The door of their flat creaked open. "*Ciao,* Mama!" Twelve-year-old Valeria walked in, followed by ten-year-old Anna, their book bags hanging from their shoulders. They dropped them to the floor and ran to embrace Maria.

Anna, always the perceptive one, gazed at Maria's face. "Mama, you've been crying!"

Maria had hoped to keep the bad news from her children, at least until she'd discussed it with Luca. "I received a telegram from *Zia* Cristina. She said that *Nonna* is very sick."

Valeria pulled up a chair and sat down next to Maria. "What's happening, Mama?"

Should she tell the children of her plans? "I must go back to Sicily for a little while. To be with *Nonna.* I want to see her before she dies." The words caught in Maria's throat.

Anna took Maria's hand. "Oh, Mama. I will go with you."

"And I will, too." Valeria brushed away a tear from Maria's face.

"I wish you could, dear ones. But there isn't enough money to pay for your tickets. Even paying for mine will be a sacrifice."

"Can we work on the ship to pay our passage?"

"I don't think that is permitted. Besides, I wouldn't want you working in that kind of environment."

Valeria stroked Maria's hand. "Maybe Nico can go with you."

At Valeria's suggestion, Maria's heart filled with hope. Having her grown son's company would be the next best thing to having Luca go with her. Result of the greatest tragedy of her life, Nico had become her focal point. On him she'd pinned every hope, every dream, every consolation for her immense suffering. Although he was the fruit of a rape, she'd vowed to show him he was a person of great worth in God's eyes, a young man with a destiny. Not the illegitimate outcast her Sicilian village of Pisano had viciously declared him to be.

She cringed at the memory.

Often, Luca would half-teasingly tell her that Nico had become a god to her. An icon of worship in human form. She'd shuddered at the thought but could not deny there was some truth to what Luca said. Over the years, she'd found herself intervening more and more in Nico's life, almost as if she owned him. Luca had accused her of possessiveness. A possessiveness spawned in the years shortly after Nico's birth, years during which she'd been alone with her son, sequestered on *Bella Terra* for fear of their being harmed by the villagers.

This precious son, whose nineteenth birthday was only a few days away, had become a grown man, with a steady job in the garment industry. A responsible young adult whose life was separate from hers, as much as Maria struggled to accept that truth.

She considered Valeria's suggestion with measured breath.

Dare she ask Nico to buy a ticket to accompany her? He'd been saving most of his earnings toward the purchase of a house for the day when he would marry. A distant goal, but one he hoped to achieve one day. She could not ask him to jeopardize his dream.

Unless she offered to pay him back every penny.

"And don't worry, Mama. We will take good care of Papa while you're gone."

"I'm sure you will." The thought of leaving Luca and the girls behind wrenched her heart. She'd never been away from them for more than a day. To be separated from them for several weeks would be unbearable.

"I know how to cook *pasta e fagioli*," Valeria offered.

"And I know how to set the table," Anna chimed in.

Maria laughed in spite of herself. "I am so blessed to have the two most wonderful daughters in the whole world." She hugged them close.

"And we're blessed to have the best mama in the whole world."

A longing tugged at Maria's heart. That's exactly how she felt about her own mama.

A mama she might never see again.

* * * *

Nico Tonetta trudged home from work as another major snowstorm pummeled Brooklyn. Already, nearly a foot of snow had fallen, and another four inches were forecast before morning. Traffic was at a standstill, with only horse-driven snowplows crawling the streets in an attempt to make them passable. Draped in heavy woolen blankets, the poor horses seemed as cold as he was.

A bitter wind whipped Nico's face, causing tears to well up in his eyes. Shivering in his thin coat, he shoved his gloveless hands more deeply into his pockets and set his gaze toward the tenement house where, at almost nineteen, he still lived with Mama, Papa, and his younger sisters, Valeria and Anna. His sisters loved the cold. Perhaps they'd left Sicily at a young enough age so as not to remember its warm, balmy climate.

He sighed. In his eight years in Brooklyn, he still hadn't grown accustomed to the cold winters.

Would he ever?

But it wasn't only the cold winter weather that made him feel like a misfit. Whenever he ventured out of his Italian neighborhood—which he did as rarely as possible—he faced jeers, slurs, and discrimination just for being Italian. Once, he'd even been beaten for daring to walk through a well-established, wealthy neighborhood on his way to the train that took him to the Manhattan clothing factory where he worked. Thank God the police had broken up the unruly gang of preppy schoolboys before they could inflict permanent physical damage on him.

Nico flinched at the memory.

As for emotional damage, no policeman could have prevented that. His muscles still tensed at the thought of the demeaning incident. Ever since, he'd taken a different route to and from the train station.

He rounded the corner that led to the street in front of his run-down tenement house. Most of the pushcart peddlers who normally greeted his return from the clothing factory every evening had already left for the day. Only one lingered, offering his fare of hot *calzoni* to any straggler brave enough to weather the elements.

Nico stopped. The poor old man seemed in need of encouragement. "One hot *calzone*, please."

The man smiled weakly. "I must warn you they are no longer hot. My heater ran out of fuel."

"No matter." Nico smiled. "I'll take it anyway. I am more hungry than cold."

The man wrapped a *calzone* in brown paper and handed it

to Nico. "God bless you, my son."

Nico handed him a few coins. "Keep the change. And God bless you, too."

A tear trickled down the old man's cheek as he pocketed the coins. His lips quivered. "*Grazie.*"

Nico's heart sank. So many Italian immigrants had come to America with hope in their hearts. Nearly half had returned to Italy disillusioned. Many of those who'd remained had discovered that any gold-paved streets they'd hoped to find would be streets they'd have to pave with their own blood, sweat, and tears.

Yet, they chose to persevere anyway, ever hopeful that things would one day change.

But would they? And what about him? Now an adult, could he make it on his own in a country the majority of whose people hated and distrusted Italians? Who looked on them as inferior beings best relegated to the pigpen?

Who allowed prejudice and pride to overrule human decency?

Truth be told, the odds were against him. The land of milk and honey Papa and Mama had imagined had turned out to be a land of sour milk and vinegar. Returning to Sicily was looking better and better.

The wind picked up as Nico approached his tenement house. The dilapidated building had aged even more in the years since his family had lived there. An eerie silence pervaded the street that normally resounded with the voices of mothers calling for their children to come in to dinner, of newspaper delivery boys hawking the day's news, and of middle-aged street musicians playing their accordions and harmonicas in the hope of earning a few pennies. The snowstorm had turned the usually noisy street into a scene of silence. Except for the lamps burning in the apartment windows, there was no sign of human life. A stray dog, covered with snow, whimpered on the street corner. Nico broke off a piece of the *calzone* and tossed it to the dog. The poor animal had barely enough strength to totter toward it and grab it between his shivering jaws.

Lifting the collar of his worn coat around his bare ears, Nico pushed solidly into the gusting wind. Only a few more yards to go before he would reach the main entrance to the tenement house. The storm had grown to nearly blizzard proportions. He looked back toward the old peddler. To Nico's relief, the man had left for home.

Thick, heavy flakes fell from the sky like shooting stars, piling atop one another as they reached the ground. Oh, for the warm sunshine of southern Sicily! His mind drifted back to the beautiful land of his birth. Although he was only eleven when he'd left, he still could picture the gently rolling hills of *Bella Terra*, his mother's family farm, with its lemon orchards, its lush vineyards, and its purple-blue mountains, majestic against the golden-orange horizon. How he missed the fragrance of the orange groves and the wild rabbits scurrying through the fields! And Pippo, the *Lagotto Romagnolo* puppy his grandmother had given him on his eleventh birthday, shortly before his departure for America. What had become of the dog? Was he still alive? Did Pippo miss him?

A surge of longing filled Nico's soul. He missed Sicily. He missed *Bella Terra*. He missed his grandmother. She'd been like a second mother to him.

And, strangely enough, he missed Don Franco Malbone. The man who'd been his first teacher at the village school, his parish priest, and the man at whose side he'd worked in the fields. The man who, as foreman of *Bella Terra*, had brought the two-hundred-year-old family farm back from the brink of bankruptcy.

The man who had wronged his mother.

Mama said she'd forgiven him years ago. For what, Nico didn't know. Beyond stating that Don Franco had greatly wronged her, Mama had told Nico nothing. As proof of her forgiveness, she'd even hired Franco to work on the family farm.

Nico's throat hitched. The same unutterable thought bombarded his mind yet again, as it had quite often of late. A frightening thought. An unbearable thought. A thought that shook him to the very roots of his being and that his mirror kept confirming every morning.

He resembled Don Franco. The same black, wavy hair. The same dark, penetrating eyes.

The same Roman nose and strong, square chin.

Not only that, but he had the short, solid build of the man, not the slender look of Mama's small frame. Only the shape of his eyes resembled Mama's.

Nico shuddered at the thought he wanted to expel more than anything else. Could he himself have anything to do with the offense for which Mama had forgiven Don Franco?

A chill shook his veins.

Could Don Franco be his biological father?

Chapter Two

Maria looked up from the worn housedress she was mending as Nico opened the door and entered the tiny flat. Her heart warmed with relief at the sight of her son. Outside, a blizzardly wind beat furiously against the balcony door, now covered thick with snow, causing it to rattle. A cold draft blew across the room, defying the heat coming from the iron stove.

"Nico, thank God you're home! I am so relieved to see you!" Maria put aside her sewing and rose to greet her son.

"*Ciao*, Mama." Nico smiled and then removed his snow-covered overcoat and hung it on the coat rack. Next, he pulled off his old leather boots and placed them to dry on the large hemp mat next to the door.

Maria extended her arms in welcome. "Praise the Lord for bringing you safely home. I was worried about you." She embraced the son who now surpassed her in height by nearly four inches.

Nico smiled at her and planted a kiss on her cheek. "You worry too much, Mama."

"That's exactly what I tell her," shouted Anna as she ran across the room to greet her older brother. "Truth be told, though, I was worried about you, too. This is a terrible snowstorm. The worst, I think, since we've been in America."

"How do you know?" Valeria challenged her younger sister. "You were only two years old when we got here."

"Girls, please!" Maria intervened. "Let's not get into an argument over a snowstorm. The point is that your brother Nico is safely home."

With a twinkle in his eye and a smile on his lips, Nico

turned to twelve-year-old Valeria. "And what about you, Valeria? Were you worried about your big brother as well?"

Valeria waved a hand in the air. "No. I never worry about anything."

Nico tousled her black, curly hair. "You are the wisest one among us then." He took a seat by the hot stove and rubbed his hands in front of it to warm them. "This cold goes right through one's bones. Makes me long for the warm climate of Sicily."

Maria's heart lurched. "Speaking of Sicily, I got a telegram from your *Zia* Cristina today."

Nico stopped rubbing his hands and looked up. "And?"

"*Nonna* is not well. I must go to her at once."

He remained silent for a moment, the way he always did when processing new information. "When will you leave?"

"I hope to leave on the next ship sailing to Sicily."

"But it's the dead of winter, Mama. The ocean will be rough and dangerous."

"I cannot let that enter into my decision. I don't know how much time *Nonna* has left." Her voice caught on the edge of a sob. "In fact, I don't even know if she is still alive. *Zia* Cristina's telegram was dated January 3rd and arrived this morning."

Nico's face grew pensive. "Will Papa go with you?"

Maria's muscles tensed. "We can afford only one round-trip ticket. If, that is, we can afford any at all."

Nico rose from the chair and moved toward Maria. "I will help you, Mama. You can have as much of my savings as you need."

"But you must keep your savings to build a house. To start a new life once you get married. I cannot, nor will I, ask you to do that."

Nico smiled faintly. "I don't even have a girlfriend yet, Mama." He placed a hand on Maria's shoulder. "Besides, I don't want you traveling alone. If Papa cannot go, I will go with you."

Relief flooded Maria's soul. Although she secretly hoped either Luca or Nico could travel with her, she dared not ask her son to make such a sacrifice. "Let me first find out from Papa what he thinks we should do. Either way, I have to think of Valeria and Anna. They will need someone to care for them."

Anna tugged on Maria's arm. "Can we stay with *Signora* Addevico, Mama?"

Anna had read Maria's mind. "Actually, I was considering asking *Signora* Addevico to care for you while I'm away. I know she would be happy to help me, since she has only Lia still living at home."

"Oh, please, Mama!" Valeria begged. "It would be so much fun!"

Over the years since they'd lived in the tenement house, Anna and Valeria had become good friends with Enza's teenaged daughter Lia and her older sister Gina, who occasionally babysat for Luca and Maria.

Maria put an arm around Valeria's shoulders. "There is a lot to think about. And to pray about. I will discuss all these things with Papa when he returns tomorrow. But for now, I will focus on getting all of us some dinner."

Having Luca gone for days at a time was very difficult for her. Although Maria was thankful her husband had a job when so many others were out of work, she missed having him home for dinner every night. Besides, she worried that the difficult conditions under which he worked—skipping meals, sleeping in unheated train cars night after night, being vulnerable to prejudicial crimes against Italians—were taking their toll on his health. At times, she wondered if moving to America had been a good idea after all. What did they have to show for their move after so many long years? Not much, if anything. Oh, yes, their brief time at the mission had produced spiritual fruit. But when the mission had closed due to lack of financial support, so had Luca's opportunity to work there.

The thought of moving back to Sicily grew more and more compelling in her mind and heart.

Heaving a sigh, Maria donned the red linen apron she'd brought with her from Sicily years earlier. The apron Mama had worn and had given to her when Maria had married, symbolizing the passing of the torch from one generation to the next. The apron was her one physical link to Mama. Her one physical link to *Bella Terra*.

It would be another long day before Luca returned from the railroad. She would need to purchase two round-trip tickets, but she would have to wait until Luca's return before doing so. It might be that he would be able to accompany her in Nico's place.

But waiting when waiting was not an option was almost impossible to do.

* * * *

Maria was still awake when Luca walked in the door just before midnight the next day. Even after nearly fourteen years of marriage, her heart still leapt at the sight of him. Careful not to awaken the children, she rushed toward the door to greet him. "Welcome home, *amore mio*! I am so glad to see you!" His face, badly in need of a shave, looked weary. His clothes, ragged and unkempt.

Luca took her into his arms and kissed her warmly. "It's so good to be home."

Maria helped him off with his coat and hung it on the wooden coat rack by the door. "Have you had anything to eat?"

"Yes, but nothing like your home cooking. I've been dreaming about it for the past week."

She smiled. "Well, then, I am about to make your dreams come true." She walked over to the oven in which she'd placed a large bowl of *pasta e fagioli* to keep warm. Next to it was a slice of broiled beefsteak and a freshly baked loaf of bread. Given their tight budget, she'd hesitated about purchasing the steak. But Luca needed his strength, and red meat once in a while would give him some.

Taking a set of potholders from a hook on the wall, she removed the bowl and the bread and placed them on the kitchen table, where she'd already set a place for Luca. "*Vieni. Mangia.*"

Luca finished washing his hands at the kitchen sink and then sat down to eat. "Let's pray."

Maria placed her hand in his. It was hard and callused, the rough hand of a hard laborer. Her heart sank. If only Luca could open his own tailor shop again. He'd be able to work indoors and not have to brave the elements of frigid winters outdoors. Would they ever have enough money for him to go into business for himself again? Would this be their lot for the rest of their lives?

Had the American dream forever slipped through their fingers?

Luca's mellow voice drew her back to the moment. "Father, thank You for Your provision. You never fail us. Thank You for watching over Maria and the children while I was gone. You are ever faithful. And thank You for my precious wife who stands by me no matter what. In Jesus' name I pray. Amen."

A twinge of guilt flooded Maria's soul. If Luca only knew she'd been thinking of asking him to leave the American "promised land" and return to Sicily.

"Amen." Maria breathed the word of agreement despite the doubt that assailed her. A doubt she pushed aside out of love for her God and her husband.

Luca began to eat. "Tell me what's been going on here."

Maria took a deep breath. "I couldn't wait for you to get home." Her voice began to quaver. "I got a telegram from

Cristina. Mama is very sick and may not have long to live."

Luca's face grew somber, but he remained silent.

"Cristina said I must come quickly." Maria wrung her hands. "In fact, I wonder if Mama is still alive since Cristina's telegram is dated January 3rd."

Luca put down his fork and took Maria's hand. "You must leave right away."

She looked up at him. "I was hoping you could go with me."

"I wish I could. You have no idea how much I wish I could. But if I leave the railroad now, I may not have a job when we get back. Besides, I would receive no pay while away. The little savings we have would not be enough to sustain our expenses for more than a couple of weeks."

Maria's heart sank to her feet. "Perhaps Nico can go with me. I really don't want to make the trip alone if I can help it."

"Have you asked him?"

"No, but he offered. He said he would use part of his savings to purchase a ticket, but I can't ask him to do that."

"You're not asking him. He's offering. Besides, we will pay him back." Luca placed his hand on hers. "I think it's a good idea to have him go with you. I would feel much better about your going with someone rather than going alone."

Maria lowered her head. "Very well. I will accept his offer. We will have to book passage tomorrow on the next ship that sets sail for Sicily. You know how quickly manifests fill up."

Luca nodded. "How long will you be gone?"

"It depends on the situation I find when I get there. If Mama has already died"—she suppressed the sob that rose to her throat—"it will be a matter of only a few days. But if Mama is still lingering, I would want to talk with her doctor about how much time he thinks she has left. Depending on what happens, I could be there for several weeks."

Luca sighed and squeezed her hands. "Stay as long as you

need to." He caressed her cheek. "I will miss you terribly, dear one." He looked toward the children, sound asleep in their beds. "What about the children? Who will take care of them?"

"I've already thought of that. I'm going to ask Enza if she can help me."

"Yes. That is a good idea. She loves them like her own children."

Hot tears stung Maria's eyes. "Luca, do you think Mama is still alive?"

He stood and drew her toward him. "I hope so, Maria. I hope so with all my heart. But I don't know for sure. One thing, however, I do know for sure. Whatever you find when you get there, the Lord will be with you."

She buried her head in her husband's chest. Luca was right. The Lord would be with her.

But right now, more than anything else, she wanted Luca to be with her as well.

Chapter Three

Don Franco Malbone stared at the large 1905 calendar hanging on the classroom wall. He'd turned away momentarily from the room full of adolescent boys seated behind him to hide the emotion that had suddenly surfaced as tears in his eyes. Such unexpected outbursts of sorrow had been occurring ever more frequently in his life of late. Was it a sign of aging? Fatigue?

Or something deeper?

His gaze zeroed in on today's date, embossed on the calendar in large block letters: January 13, 1905.

Nico's nineteenth birthday.

He swallowed the throbbing ache at the back of his throat. Every year on this date, a profound heaviness of heart overwhelmed him. Yes, God had forgiven him of his horrendous sin, but some of its consequences still remained.

Like losing the presence of his son in his life.

Eight years had passed since Franco had bid farewell to then eleven-year-old Nico and taken the job as headmaster of a private boarding school in Milano. But not a day went by that he did not think of his beloved son. Not a day went by that Franco did not wish that Nico were a part of his life. As much as he'd longed to write to his son, Franco had refrained. Although he was Nico's biological father, Luca was his true father. The man who had reared him as his own. What right did Franco have to intrude into that sacred relationship?

He'd never told Nico the truth about their biological connection. Not that he had not wanted to. But that was for Maria to do, if and when she deemed appropriate.

Had she deemed it so?

He raked his fingers through his hair. Nico was a young man now. Perhaps established in a trade. Or pursuing his studies. Would he even remember the priest who'd been his first teacher and beside whom he'd tended the fields of *Bella Terra*?

Don Franco sighed. Some things in life were better laid to rest.

But some things in life defied laying to rest.

"*Professore!*" A young man's voice caught Franco's attention. "Please excuse me, sir, but, did you hear my question?"

Franco abruptly turned and shook his head. "I'm sorry, Matteo. My mind wandered for a moment. What was your question?"

Snickers came from the back of the classroom of boys as their eyes darted from one to another, full of ridicule at their teacher's seemingly senile behavior. At any other time, Franco would have been annoyed. But today, he was too weary to care.

Matteo spoke. "My question is *How do I reconcile the faith in which I was reared with the fact that such faith does not correspond to my experience of life?*"

Franco rubbed his forehead, not so much from the lack of an adequate response to the student's question but from his inability to focus today on anything other than Nico. "You ask a very valid question. Let me respond by asking you another one. What is the logical conclusion of making your personal experience of life the starting point of philosophy? Would not doing so result in faulty reasoning since you are beginning from yourself as the center of the universe rather than from God?"

Another student raised his hand. "But, *Professore*, how can one start from any point other than oneself? I know and perceive truth only through the lenses of my own being."

Franco sighed. Oh, the folly of youth! So easily embracing the latest philosophical fad without thinking it through to its logical conclusions. "But, if that were the case, then each one of us would have a different starting point and, therefore, a different conclusion. And, if a different conclusion, then a different truth. Each one of us would be our own god. This would lead to moral and political anarchy."

Matteo responded. "I disagree, *Professore*. I would suggest it would lead to more freedom since each person would be free to live as he chose."

Franco drew in a deep breath. "What would that look like in practical terms? Such a position would imply there can be freedom without responsibility. And freedom, by its very nature, implies responsibility."

Before the student could respond, the bell sounded, signaling the end of the Friday morning class hour. "We will resume this most important discussion on Monday. You are dismissed."

As the boys picked up their books and noisily left the classroom, Franco turned his gaze toward the large casement window overlooking the lawn. The beautiful campus of the medieval boarding school, nestled in a thickly wooded area just outside Milano, was covered with snow. Along the edges of the slate roof, long icicles hung solidly in ragged formation under a gray sky, without threat of melting soon, so bitter was the cold. A single swallow sat atop the roof. Was it frozen or simply resting from its flight against the wind?

Franco's gaze shifted. Across the large expanse of land, along the horizon, a single, wide row of cypress trees separated the academy's isolated campus from the rest of the world. Like Giacomo Leopardi in his classic poem *L'Infinito*, Franco longed to leave the confines of this boarding-school campus where he'd spent the last eight years of his life in near seclusion. At first, it had been good to return to teaching after a long hiatus as a farmhand. But now, he longed to escape the tedium of his daily life and to explore what lay beyond it.

Truth be told, he longed to see Nico again.

An ache pierced his heart. He turned away from the window toward the empty classroom. Perhaps he'd make a trip to America at the close of the school year.

But should he? Would it be to Nico's benefit to see his biological father again? Would the boy even want to see him? What if Maria had never told Nico the truth about their relationship?

And what about Maria? Yes, she'd forgiven him and even allowed him to work on her family farm. But would she want him intruding into her new life in America?

Intruding into their son's life?

Tumultuous doubts wrestled with one another as he turned from the window, pulled the pendant light chain, and shut the classroom door behind him.

* * * *

Four weeks later, with Nico at her side, Maria stood at the ship's railing as the *Perugia* entered Palermo harbor. The three-week Atlantic crossing had been rough and stormy, making her seasick for much of the trip. Now, at the end of it, she breathed a long sigh of relief.

Despite the unhappy reason for her return, her soul stirred at being back in her homeland. Truth be told, in her heart she'd never left. Sicily would always be an integral part of who she was. How often, during the past several years in Brooklyn, she'd longed for *Bella Terra*! Yes, her family farm had been named well: *Beautiful Land*. And she was eager to see it again.

She scanned the large crowds of people lining the shore, awaiting the arrival of loved ones. Shielding her eyes from the bright noonday sun, Maria searched for her sister Cristina and her brother-in-law Pietro. Cristina said she'd be wearing a red dress so Maria could easily spot her. As Maria's gaze searched the crowd, her heart leapt when she noticed Cristina waving frantically for her attention.

Maria waved back and then turned to Nico. "There's *Zia* Cristina!" Maria pointed toward her younger sister and Nico's aunt. "Hurry! Let's move toward the gangplank. I want to disembark before the crowd surge."

"*Sì*, Mama." Nico picked up the two suitcases they had brought with them and turned toward the gangplank.

Maria followed closely behind. The cool breeze caressing her face was a far cry from the frigid wind she'd left behind in Brooklyn. It was good to be back home. But now she must get to Mama as quickly as possible.

A lump caught in her throat. If, that is, Mama were still alive.

All around Maria, passengers hastened toward the gangplank. A crew member urged them to take their time and disembark in an orderly fashion. From the shore, shouts of welcome filled the air as weary passengers moved toward their waiting loved ones. Tears flowed and hugs abounded as families reunited.

"Mama, I see *Zia* Cristina! She's over there." Nico pointed to the right of the ship where Cristina and her husband Pietro ran toward them.

Maria's heart melted. She ran off the gangplank toward her waiting sister and, with tear-filled eyes, fell into her embrace. "Oh, Cristina! My precious Cristina! How happy I am to see you!"

Maria held her sister for a long moment, releasing the pent-up emotion of long years of absence. Then, taking both her hands, she glanced at Cristina's rounding belly. "Pregnancy becomes you!" She studied her sister's tear-stained face. "You are even more beautiful than when I left you."

Cristina chuckled, pointing to the single strand of graying hair that lined her forehead. "And you, dear Maria, look only a wee bit older." Ever the humorous one of the family, Cristina turned to Nico. "You left a little boy, and now you are a man."

Tears spilled from her eyes as Cristina warmly embraced her nephew.

Maria turned toward Pietro. "My dear brother-in-law! It is so good to see you!"

"Likewise, Maria." Pietro gave her a welcoming hug.

Cristina then took Maria's arm and entwined it in her own as they moved away from the dock. "I know you are wondering about Mama."

Maria's breath caught. Should she brace herself for the worst?

Cristina stopped short and faced her. "Mama is still alive"—her sister's voice hitched—"but she has only a very short time to live. I think you made it home just in time."

Maria's body melted into relief while her heart clutched in sorrow.

She walked arm in arm with Cristina, catching up on the news of the past eight years, while Nico and Pietro followed behind. "Is Mama still at *Bella Terra*?"

"Where else would she be? Nothing can move her from there. She vowed she would never die anywhere except at *Bella Terra*."

Maria sighed. "I can't say I blame her. *Bella Terra* has been her whole life."

"She is so eager to see you, Maria. Ever since she got sick, she's been praying fervently that you would come home before she died. Life has been difficult for her since you left." There was no condemnation in Cristina's voice. Only sadness.

Maria's heart sank. Even now, she wondered if she and Luca had made a huge mistake by leaving Sicily for the American promised land. Had they remained at *Bella Terra*, they could have enjoyed Mama's final years with her. And Mama would have been able to watch her grandchildren grow up.

Maria's stomach knotted.

Forget those things that are behind, dear one. Press forward to those things that lie ahead. The Lord's gentle, loving voice brought her to her senses. They'd done what the Lord had told them to do. That was all that mattered. She couldn't change the past. She could only commit it into the Lord's hands, trusting He had led them and would reward them for their obedience.

But what lay ahead?

Only time would tell. For now, she needed to get to Mama as quickly as possible. "We'd better hurry." Pietro's voice interrupted Maria's thoughts. "Our train for Ribera leaves in half an hour."

Soon Maria found herself seated between Cristina and Nico on a train like the one she'd ridden eight years earlier on their way to America. Little had changed. Passengers chatted, chickens squawked, and the smells of squid and clams from the nearby Mediterranean Sea filtered through the open windows. The only thing that was different the first time was the weather. They'd left in the sweltering heat of late summer, whereas now the February weather was much cooler.

She turned to Nico sitting beside her. "You were only eleven years old the last time we rode this train. Do you remember?"

He nodded. "I remember it well. I was heartbroken about leaving Pippo."

Maria placed a hand on her son's. "Yes, I, too, remember it well. My heart ached for you. I can only imagine how difficult it was to leave your puppy."

Nico looked at her with eager eyes. "Do you think he's still alive?"

Although her son was a man, she could still see the little boy in him. "He may very well be. *Lagotto Romagnolos* live between fifteen and seventeen years."

A broad grin lit Nico's face. "If Pippo is still alive, do you think he will remember me?"

"I'm sure of it. Once a dog has your scent, he never forgets it."

Nico smiled—a smile that warmed her heart. Would leaving the dog behind a second time break her son's heart yet again?

Worse yet, what if Nico didn't want to return to America?

Her muscles tensed. Where did that impossible thought come from? She chided herself for even thinking it. Nico's future was in the New World. There was no way he would remain in Sicily—especially not for a dog.

The three-hour train ride passed quickly, filled as it was with Maria's intense conversation with Cristina, catching up on the news of the past several years, while Nico engaged in lively conversation with his *Zio* Pietro seated across the aisle.

As the train neared the Ribera station, Cristina leaned toward Maria and smiled. "Salvatore is waiting for us at the station with the wagon. We should be at *Bella Terra* by dusk."

Salvatore. The old farmhand who'd taken them to the station that crazy morning of their departure for America when, for a short while, they couldn't find Nico. The boy had hidden with his puppy to avoid having to leave the dog behind.

"I didn't know Salvatore still worked at *Bella Terra.* He must be in his late sixties by now."

Cristina smiled. "He just turned seventy last month."

Maria raised an eyebrow in surprise and then gazed out the window at the fields that lay barren and dry. Just like her heart. Until now, she hadn't realized how barren her life in Brooklyn had been. Returning to Sicily had awakened a need within her. A need for connection. A connection she had not yet experienced in America, even after long and difficult years of living there.

She and Luca had occasionally discussed the possibility of returning to Sicily, but Luca had always been adamant about remaining in Brooklyn. Were it not for him and their children, she herself had no good reason to remain there.

Unless, that is, the Lord had other plans.

Chapter Four

Shortly before dawn, Don Franco walked across the snow-covered lawn of the Classical Academy for Boys just outside Milano. A stark silence hovered over the campus as the last vestiges of night melted into a new day. In the distance, the foothills of the Alps sloped upward toward snow-capped peaks, majestic and serene.

The February air was cold and damp, sending a chill through Franco's aching bones. At forty-eight years of age, his body was beginning to feel the passing of years. He wrapped his woolen scarf around his neck and lowered the front brim of his hat as he pressed into the wind.

He drew in a deep breath of the cold air. Today, he would initiate a classroom discussion on the topic of evolution that was fast sweeping across Italy, Europe, and the entire world. Ever since Darwin's publication of *The Origin of the Species* back in 1859, world culture had embarked on a path of thinking that contradicted the laws of logic and the laws of faith he held dear. Academia, especially, seemed to have lost its way in a maze of flimsy premises that, if followed to their logical conclusions, defied logic itself. This new generation of students accepted Darwinism without so much as an intellectual fight and held on to its tenets with a tight fist. Unfortunately for him, he had little strength left at his age to refute a roomful of male adolescents bent on proving him wrong.

But refute them he must. Not only for the sake of his job, but, most importantly, for the sake of Truth. Truth that, many years earlier, had set him free.

Franco thrust the key into the lock of the main door of the sixteenth-century building. The thick, heavy oaken door creaked open, as it did every morning upon his arrival. How many times had it creaked during its nearly three hundred years of existence?

He entered the dark building, lit only by the first rays of sunlight creeping up over the horizon, and pulled the door closed behind him. The ancient edifice smelled of must, mildew, and mold. A long, dark corridor led from the front door to the classroom area. To Franco's surprise, a dim light shone from the classroom straight ahead. *His* classroom.

Strange. No one else but Luigi, the custodian, had a key to the building. Perhaps he was cleaning the classroom.

Franco made his way to his classroom and peered through the glass panel on the door. Matteo sat at one of the desks, his head buried in his hands.

Franco opened the door and entered. "Matteo?"

The boy looked up. His eyes were red and swollen. "*Signor* Luigi let me in."

Franco approached the boy's side and put a hand on his shoulder. "What is the matter, son?"

"I just received word that my father has died." The boy's jaw trembled as he spoke the words.

A rush of compassion flooded Franco's heart. He sat down at the desk next to Matteo. "I am so very sorry."

Matteo looked at him, the windows of his soul darkened with grief. "I know it is your habit to come to the classroom early to prepare for the lesson, so I came early, too, hoping to find you. I want to tell you that I will be leaving the academy for a few days to be with my family and attend my father's funeral."

"Of course." Franco's heart yearned to take the boy into his arms to comfort him. "Is there anything I can do for you?"

"No. Thank you." Matteo lowered his eyes and then raised

them again. "I want to apologize for the disrespectful way in which I have treated you in class. My father would not have approved."

"All is forgiven. Just focus now on comforting your mother and your siblings." Franco swallowed hard, remembering his own pain when his father died. "I will be praying for you." He stood, sensing the boy's discomfort.

"Thank you." Matteo rose. He lingered for a moment and then awkwardly gave Franco a quick embrace. In an instant, he was out the door.

With a saddened heart, Franco watched the boy leave. Would Nico be as distraught when Franco died? Would Nico even care? No father-son relationship had developed between them. Impossible, given the situation. Yes, there had been a teacher-pupil relationship, but for a short time only. And Nico had worked alongside Franco at *Bella Terra*, bringing in the harvest. But their conversations had been generic. Never deep or intimate, such as those between a father and his son.

Franco shuddered. An overwhelming longing to see his son flooded Franco's soul. He rose and walked toward the large casement window overlooking the lawn. The morning sun peeked over the horizon, its rays splitting in all directions as it rose over the distant trees. He must see Nico again. He must tell him how much he loved him. He must ask Nico's forgiveness for the grave harm he'd inflicted upon Maria, Nico's mother. He must do this as soon as possible. Tomorrow was not guaranteed to anyone. He must not die before seeing his son. Only in this way could Franco die in peace.

"Lord," he whispered. "Make a way for me to see my Nico again. Please, Lord. I want him to know how much I love him. I want to ask him to forgive me."

He swallowed a sob. "When my time comes, I want to die in peace, knowing my son loves me."

* * * *

As the wagon traveled the winding dirt road that led up the hill to *Bella Terra*, Nico's heart swelled. The sight of the farm's terraced hills took him back in time, while a gentle breeze swept across his face. Fond memories of his childhood on the family farm flooded his soul. Suddenly, the intervening years in America disappeared as he pictured himself running through the fields of *Bella Terra*, chasing rabbits and butterflies. Climbing the gnarled, fruit-laden olive tree on the south side of the villa. Catching trout with his bare hands in the narrow stream that ran at the bottom of the hill behind the house.

He sighed. Why had his parents left this paradise? What would his life have been like had they remained in Sicily?

Where was God in all of this?

Nico turned toward his mother sitting next to him. Her face was taut with the prospect of seeing her own dying mother after several years of separation. "Mama, are you all right?"

Maria looked at him and smiled weakly. "Yes, *figlio mio*."

He was *her* son, at least.

She patted his hand. "I'm just nervous about how I will find your *Nonna*. *Zia* Cristina says she has little time left to live."

"Do you think *Nonna* will recognize me?"

Maria's gaze locked with his. "I'm certain she will. Even though you've grown into a fine young man, your features are still your own."

Were his features someone else's, too?

Dare he ask Mama the question that burned in his soul? The question that had haunted him for some time now?

The question that shouted at him every morning when he looked in the mirror?

He drew in a deep breath. Now was not the time to ask. Soon they would arrive at *Bella Terra*, and Mama would be preoccupied with many things. But he could not delay asking much longer. He needed to know who he really was. He must know the truth about his father. He must know if his suspicions about Don Franco were well-founded or only fantasies of his imagination.

The wagon pulled up behind the house and in front of the veranda. Everything looked just as Nico had left it, except the trees were taller and the house more weather-worn.

And *Nonna* was missing from her rocking chair on the back porch.

He swallowed hard.

The wagon came to a full stop. As Nico alighted, the twittering warble of a barn swallow greeted his ears. His gaze followed the sound and discovered the lovely creature with cobalt feathers and tawny breast perched on the weather vane attached to the roof of the old barn.

Nico extended his hand to help Mama descend from the wagon. "We're finally here."

"Yes." She held his hand tightly, more—he was certain—for his moral support than his physical strength.

Zio Pietro helped *Zia* Cristina descend, after which Salvatore unhitched the horse and led the old mare to the barn.

"Are you ready?" *Zia* Cristina turned toward them and posed the question that had been on Nico's heart. Was one ever ready to face the imminent death of a loved one?

But which was worse? Losing a loved one whom one had known, or losing an identity one had never known?

Chapter Five

Her arm locked onto Nico's, Maria braced herself and followed Cristina and Pietro into the house. The once boisterous kitchen, filled with the family's laughter, was now dark and silent. Mama's old navy blue apron hung on the same hook by the iron stove. She wouldn't be wearing it again. In the corner of the room, the old high chair in which Nico, Valeria, and Anna had eaten their first meals now stood empty, waiting to be filled by Cristina and Pietro's soon-to-be-born child.

A child who most likely would not know his *Nonna*.

Maria followed Cristina and Pietro up the stairs to Mama's bedroom on the second floor. Maria's heart raced at the prospect of what she would find. Would that she'd visited when Mama was still well! When happy memories could have been forged. When laughter would have resounded throughout the ancient homestead. Maria didn't want to remember Mama as dying, but as the vibrant, energetic woman she'd always been.

A moan came from Mama's bedroom as they reached the top of the stairs.

Maria's heart clenched.

Cristina placed a hand on Maria's arm. "She's been in pain for the last several weeks. I know she will be so very happy to see you."

Tears rushed to Maria's eyes, slipping onto her cheeks. Every muscle in her body stood at heightened attention, bracing for the worst.

Cristina stopped at the doorway, a solemn look on her face, and motioned for Maria to enter first.

Her heart pounding, Maria walked into the room, Nico

following close behind her. At the sight of Mama lying on the bed, frail and broken, Maria burst into tears. She ran to Mama's side. "Oh, Mama! Mama! Mama!" She leaned over and carefully embraced her mother, holding on to her for several long moments.

The old woman tried to raise herself up on one arm, but to no avail. Her weakness would not permit it.

She spoke through trembling lips. *"Figlia mia."* Mama wrapped her bony fingers around Maria's hand. "Now that you've come, I can die in peace."

A lump formed in Maria's throat. "No, Mama. No! It's not time for you to die." Somehow. saying the words gave Maria a strange sense of control over the circumstances, a desperate power over the situation. But, in the depths of her soul, she knew otherwise.

Maria straightened and then, extending her arm toward Nico, she motioned him toward the bed. "Mama, look who is here with me."

Mama's gaze followed Maria's gesture. A gasp rose from Mama's lips. "Glory to God! Nico! My precious Nico!" She extended her emaciated arm, lined with bulging blue veins, toward her grandson and grabbed his hand. "Now I can truly die in peace, for the Lord has granted me this bonus blessing. The gift of seeing my grandson once again." Her voice quavered as she spoke the words.

Nico approached the bed and smiled. *"Ciao, Nonna!"* He bent over and embraced her, planting a gentle kiss on her wrinkled cheek. "I am so happy I could come."

She clung to his hand. "You have made your old *Nonna* very, very happy."

Maria wiped the perspiration from Mama's forehead. "Don't think of dying, Mama. Think of getting better."

Mama's gaze penetrated Maria's soul. "My precious daughter, there is an appointed time for everyone to leave this earth.

My time is fast approaching."

It was of no use. Mama had made up her mind she was going to die soon. Nothing Maria could say or do would change that fact. The only thing that remained was to enjoy as much time as possible with her before she died.

Mama turned her gaze toward her firstborn. "You are as beautiful as ever." Tears welled up in her eyes. "Oh, how I have missed you! How I have longed for the day when I would see you again!" The tears now rolled, one after another, down Mama's cheeks.

"Well, that day has finally come, Mama. Here I am." Her heart heavy, Maria forced a smile.

Mama patted the bed. "Come, sit here next to me, and tell me how you're doing." She managed a weak smile.

Maria sat on the old bed, careful not to disturb Mama's little comfort in any way.

Maria squeezed Mama's hand. "You already know much of what we've been doing these past eight years. I tried to keep you updated through my letters." A sob caught in Maria's throat. "One thing I can tell you is that I've missed you terribly. More than any letter could ever convey."

Mama's lower lip quivered. "I've missed you, too, my dear daughter." Mama struggled to speak. "Are you happy living in America?"

Should Maria tell Mama how she really felt about living in America? How she and Luca had struggled—and continued to struggle—in a land that did, indeed, offer opportunity, but at the very high cost of suffering, prejudice, and pain? How she really wished she'd never left Sicily? No. Better to keep her suffering to herself. Mama had enough suffering of her own. "We are faring well, Mama, despite some setbacks."

"Setbacks?" Mama's face grew concerned. "Setbacks like what? Did you not find the streets of gold that everyone talks about?"

A weight fell on Maria's heart. As heavy as the asphalt of which America's streets were really made. She regretted having spoken the word. "The so-called streets of gold are *potentially* there, but one must work very hard to pave them with gold." She rubbed Mama's hand. "But until one does, the streets are made of sweat and tears and plain hard work."

Mama only nodded, her eyes revealing a deep regret for the time lost between them. Time they could have spent enjoying each other. Time Mama could have spent watching her grandchildren grow. "And Luca, Valeria, and Anna? How are they?"

"They are growing fast and speak fluent English."

"That's wonderful, but I hope they don't forget our beautiful Italian language."

Maria reassured Mama they would not. "As for Luca, he works very hard on the railroad." She didn't tell Mama of Luca's continual struggle to succeed in a land that offered little mercy to Italians. "God is working things out for our good."

"Yes, God always works things out for our good when we love Him and are in His will."

Relief flooded Maria's soul. After all these years, Mama had finally come to grips with their decision to go to America. A decision Mama had anguished over for a long, long time. "Yes, that's the whole point, Mama. Luca and I have been in God's will, even though it has been hard on all of us, especially you."

Mama's gaze pierced Maria's soul. "Your absence has taught me much about the Lord, Maria. I have learned that His ways are higher than our ways and His thoughts higher than our thoughts."

"I am still learning that, Mama." Would she ever learn that lesson completely? "Can you get up from the bed at all? Perhaps we can take you outside into the fresh air to watch the sunset."

"Pietro and Salvatore carry me outside on a pallet a few

times a week. They put me on the back veranda, where I can take my fill of the beautiful countryside of *Bella Terra*."

"Would you like them to carry you there now? Salvatore is in the barn, wiping down the horse. We can ask him to help us before he retires for the day."

Mama smiled. "Yes. Yes, I would like that very much. We can sit on the back veranda, the way we used to do so many years ago. It will be like old times."

Did Maria notice a spark of life in Mama's dark eyes? Had seeing her daughter again invigorated her? Renewed her hope?

Given her a reason for living?

In a few moments, she and Mama were settled on the back veranda as the sun made its lovely descent into the western horizon. Brilliant bands of crimson, gold, and purple stretched across a cloudless blue sky that was not hidden by tenement houses, smokestacks, or elevated trains. Only mountains rested against it, adding to its unspeakable beauty and majesty.

Maria took in a deep breath. Yes, deep. All the way down to the bottom of her lungs. The kind of breath she could not take in Brooklyn. The fresh, pure air of *Bella Terra* filled her with life. The kind of life that comes only from living in the country.

Indeed, how had she survived without this land that gave her that life?

A deep longing filled Maria's soul. A longing to return to this beautiful land of her birth. The land of her roots.

The land of her upbringing.

But Luca would never be willing.

She looked at Mama, propped up against a pillow on the pallet beside her, serene and content. If Luca could see Mama now, would he consider moving back?

If Maria ever doubted anything in her life, she doubted this.

* * * *

Mama slipped away peacefully, at the crack of dawn a few days later, surrounded by Maria, Maria's two younger sisters Cristina and Luciana, Cristina's husband Pietro, and Nico.

The sun's first bright rays of the new day filtered through the white lace curtains of Mama's bedroom window. Perched on the windowsill, a brown, white-streaked song sparrow sang a doleful tribute to the lady of the house who had just died.

Maria sat at Mama's bedside, praying and holding her hand. The hand that had caressed her face when she was but a child. The hand that had wiped her brow when she'd been hot with fever. The hand that had given her a gentle swat on the bottom when she'd disobeyed.

Numbness settled in Maria's bones. The woman she'd called "Mama" all her life now lay lifeless on her bed of affliction. "She's gone." She whispered the final words to Cristina, who stood close beside her. "I came back just in time." A shudder went through her. "Just in time to spend her last few days with her."

A sob caught in Maria's throat and then unleashed itself into a torrent of tears. She buried her face on Mama's breast, wailing in lament at the loss of the woman who had given her life and had been her life.

Then, turning to Cristina, Maria fell onto her sister's shoulder, and the two of them wept, holding each other in their bitter anguish.

Finally, Maria raised her head, tasting the bitter, salty tears that had settled on her lips. "We have to make arrangements."

"They've already been made." Cristina took Maria's hands into her own. "Mama knew she was going to die. She planned her funeral ahead of time, so that we would not have to think about anything."

"Except grieving." The word now held new meaning for her. Papa's death had generated overwhelming grief in her heart. A grief that still lingered, even after more than two decades. But losing Mama was a different kind of grief. A grief whose roots lay in the womb and in the mighty bond initially forged there between mother and child.

"I will notify the rectory to schedule the funeral. We will also need to notify our relatives and friends."

Maria's head spun. Thankful that Cristina had her wits about her, Maria turned to Nico. "Are you all right, son?"

Tears trickled down the boy's cheeks. This was the first death in the family he'd experienced. He'd never known Maria's father, having been born after his grandfather's death. "*Nonna* was a wonderful woman." The words caught in Nico's throat.

Maria placed an arm around her son's shoulders. "And she loved you so very much."

"I wish I'd been able to grow up near her."

The words stung. Regret flooded Maria's soul. Nico had echoed the very sentiments of her own heart. What harm had she inflicted upon her children in leaving Sicily? Of what wonderful experiences with their grandmother had she robbed them by moving to America?

How deeply had she broken Mama's heart by removing her precious grandchildren from her?

Cristina covered Mama's body with the bedsheet. "I have sent Salvatore to fetch the priest and the mortician. They will be here shortly." Maria was thankful for her sister's busy resourcefulness. It was Cristina's way of numbing her own pain.

"Very well. What can I do in the meanwhile?"

Cristina's tear-filled eyes gazed at her with love. "Why don't you just sit by Mama's bedside until they get here. I think it will make you feel better."

Did Cristina grasp the intense guilt Maria felt at not having been here the last eight years? Did she realize that while she herself had spent that time enjoying their mother, Maria had missed this great blessing?

Cristina and Pietro left the room, leaving Maria and Nico to themselves.

Nico solemnly approached Maria. "Mama, would you mind if I walked out in the fields for a while?"

"No, my son. Not at all."

"Thank you. I feel the need to be alone."

How well she understood that need! It was a need she'd shared many times during the bitter days after she'd discovered she was pregnant out of wedlock.

"May the Lord comfort you as you walk."

Nico nodded and then, without saying a word, he left.

Maria was now alone with Mama. But, truth be told, Mama had left, too. Her spirit had soared through the heavens and now stood before the Savior and Lord she'd loved all of her life. Jesus Christ, the King of Kings!

So, Maria was all alone. Wondering what Mama was seeing now. Rejoicing at her wholeness now.

Marveling at her freedom from all pain and sorrow.

Would that she, too, could experience that same freedom! One day she would. But for now, she was confined to the realm of earth, called to complete a purpose of which she was growing more and more uncertain each day.

Chapter Six

His hands shoved into his pockets, Nico made his way across the fields of *Bella Terra*. A brilliant sun shone high in a cloudless blue sky, extending its warm rays over the countryside. The terraced hills smelled of ripening citrus. Beneath his feet, the rich soil yielded readily to his footprints, covering his boots with its fine dust.

Nico's eyes scanned the beautiful landscape. It invigorated not only his body but also his soul. A yearning to remain in this land of his birth overtook him.

His mind drifted back to the many happy days he'd spent roaming these hillsides. Days of boyhood freedom. Days of exploration and adventure.

Days of joy.

In the distance, the emerald green Mediterranean Sea glimmered against the purple hills. He took a deep breath of the fresh salt air, a far cry from the smoke-filled atmosphere of Brooklyn. Although still cool, the temperature in early February was a welcome respite from the frigid temperatures of his American city. The sun's rays caressed his face—and his heart as well.

Surprisingly, being back in Sicily had stirred emotions long forgotten. Despite the sad reason for the visit, his heart soared with new life.

Or was it with life long buried?

Slowly and carefully, he descended the gravel path that separated the bare vineyards on one side from the lemon orchards on the other. To his right, rows and rows of lemon trees, laden with fragrant, ripening *primofiore invernale* lemons offered hope that the days of drought were finally over and that Sicily's economy would soon turn around. To Nico's left, empty grape arbors stood like sentinels, waiting for the luscious grapes that would bloom come summer. Just ahead of him, a group of strong-muscled farm laborers, bent over in concentrated effort, busily prepared for the imminent orange harvest. As they worked, they hummed in unison an old Sicilian folk song Nico had often heard as a child. He began to hum with them.

Suddenly, Nico stopped short as a wiry, chestnut-colored dog rushed out from the lemon grove onto the path in front of him and began sniffing his boots. The dog wagged his tail as though greeting a long-lost friend.

Nico stooped to pet him, his eyes studying the delightful creature. Recognition stirred in Nico's soul. No! It couldn't be! Or could it? Was the eager dog sniffing at his boots his very own Pippo, the puppy he'd left behind eight years earlier? But the creature was no longer a puppy. He was a beautiful, full-grown *Lagotto Romagnolo*.

Nico rubbed the dog's head. "Pippo? Is it really you?" He cupped the dog's snout in his hands and gazed into his eyes. A warm sensation flooded Nico's soul. Yes, it was Pippo! Unmistakably. Nico would recognize those eyes anywhere.

He picked up the dog and crushed him to his heart. Tears stung Nico's eyes. A deep-seated, subconscious longing rose to the surface of his soul. After all these years, he still grieved leaving his puppy.

Squealing with delight, Pippo licked Nico's face while wiggling for joy in his old master's arms.

Nico buried his face in the dog's neck. "Oh, Pippo! I can't believe it's you!"

Just then a young man walked up the path. "So, there you are, Pippo. I've been looking all over for you."

Nico stood and greeted the man. "Is this your dog?"

"Well, let's just say I've adopted him. His owner moved to

America several years ago, and *Signora* Landro asked me to raise the pup. The dog belonged to her grandson Nico." The man extended a callused hand. "I'm Roberto. I'm a farmhand here at *Bella Terra*."

Nico smiled. "And I'm Nico."

The man's eyes widened in surprise. "So, you are Nico! Salvatore told me you had come from America." Roberto extended his hand. "*Un miracolo!*"

Nico laughed. "I agree. It is a miracle. Thank you so much for taking care of Pippo all these years."

"It has been my great pleasure, I assure you. Pippo is a magnificent dog." Roberto petted the dog on the head. "I see he hasn't forgotten you." His voice was wistful.

Nico nodded, his heart warming. "And I haven't forgotten him." He planted a kiss on the dog's forehead. "Not for one second."

The man's eyes were compassionate. "So, you are here to visit your grandmother."

"Yes." Nico hesitated. "She just died."

"Oh, I am so sorry!" Tears welled up in his eyes.

"Thank you. Mama and I arrived just in time."

Roberto nodded. "Your *Nonna* was a wonderful woman. Hardly a day went by that she did not speak of you."

A lump rose to Nico's throat.

"She would often remark how she hoped to see you and your family again before she died." His words were meant to comfort, not condemn.

"I'm so glad Mama and I were able to spend her last days with her."

Roberto paused a moment. "Will you be taking Pippo back with you to America?"

Nico did not miss the quaver in the man's voice. "As much as I want to, I'm afraid not. Pets are not permitted onboard ship." He hugged Pippo close. "I will have to leave him yet again. Besides, it would be cruel to remove him from the only world he's ever known."

Roberto smiled. "Truth be told, I have grown to love him as my own dog. I will continue to take good care of him for you. I promise."

"What can I do to repay you?"

A look of surprise crossed Roberto's face. "Repay me? Having Pippo by my side is payment enough."

Nico smiled. "Where do you live?"

The man pointed to a distant cottage. "Over there. In the farmhands' quarters. Only two of us remain on a full-time basis. The rest are hired by the day, as needed."

Nico drew in a deep breath. "Are things very bad on the farm?"

The man lowered his gaze and then raised it again. "Let's say it's been very difficult for your grandmother. But she refused to sell the farm. She would often say *Bella Terra* was her home and she would die here."

"Did she worry that the farm would be sold after her death?"

"If she did, she never mentioned it. But your *Zia* Cristina once told me that your *Nonna's* heart would break if the farm were ever sold."

"Do you know if *Zia* Cristina is planning to sell now that *Nonna* has died?"

The man nodded. "I believe the plan is to sell the farm. It has become too much to care for in the current economic climate. As you know, Sicily has virtually collapsed financially." The man rubbed his chin. "But one must do what one must do."

A thought crossed Nico's mind. What if he returned to Sicily to take over the family farm? It would be his way of continuing the two-hundred-year-old family legacy. A fitting way to honor his grandmother. A way to make it up to her for leaving.

Perhaps, even, a gift to his own mother.

Excitement for the idea mounted in his heart. He had nothing to lose. And, perhaps, something to gain. He had not yet permanently established himself in any trade in America. Now would be as good a time as any to make a big move.

Roberto sighed. "It would be a shame to let *Bella Terra* leave the family's hands after almost two hundred years." Roberto's gaze locked onto Nico's. "Why don't you take over the farm?"

Nico's heart lurched. "The thought went through my mind."

"Well, then, don't dismiss it. Think about it seriously. It may be that God is calling you to return to Sicily."

"Thank you. I will think about it." Nico extended a hand to Roberto. "But God will have to make a way."

Roberto extended his hand in return. "Well, I must get back to work. It was a pleasure to meet you, Nico." He glanced at Pippo. "And if you ever do return to *Bella Terra*, Pippo is yours. No questions asked."

Nico heartily shook Roberto's hand. "Thank you, my friend. Pippo has enough love for both of us."

Roberto smiled. Then, taking Pippo from Nico, he returned to the fields from whence he had come.

Shielding his eyes from the bright sun, Nico followed the pair, his heart filling with nostalgia.

For him to purchase *Bella Terra* would take a miracle of the first order.

* * * *

On the day of Mama's funeral, the house buzzed with the chatter of family and friends. The church service had been brief but meaningful, and now everyone had gathered at *Bella Terra* for the traditional funeral repast. Neighbors from near and far had come, bringing with them large plates of pasta, baskets of homemade bread and pastries, and platters of roasted chicken and beef.

Dazed by the wrenching events of the past week, Maria moved among the guests, doing her best to receive with grace their heartfelt condolences and comfort. Many among them were those who had shunned her several years earlier, when she'd been found with child.

With Nico.

Out of wedlock.

She flinched at the memory. But the bitterness was gone. Only compassion remained. Proof that she'd truly forgiven them.

She entered the large parlor at the front of the house and stopped short. Her heart lurched. There before her, chatting with Nico, stood Don Franco. His presence surprised her yet made sense. He'd known Mama for many years, first as his parishioner and then as his employer during the years he'd worked as a farmhand at *Bella Terra* after his defrocking. He'd grown to love Mama dearly.

Maria took a deep breath and entered the room.

Don Franco turned and smiled.

His eyes were kind and pure, not the lustful eyes that had once terrified her with their deep-seated evil.

Nico approached Maria and took her by the elbow. "Mama, look who's here." Yes. Don Franco Malbone. The man who'd ruined her life—or so she'd thought. The man whom God had used to teach her the truth about forgiveness. The truth about the way God works all things for the good of those who love Him.

For an instant, she studied the former prelate. All bitterness toward him was gone. She approached him and extended a hand. "Don Franco, thank you so much for coming. It's a long way from Milano."

"Maria, it is such a blessing to see you." He kissed her on

both cheeks. "Of course, I came. I could not have done otherwise. When I was notified of your mother's passing, I left immediately."

The intervening years had taken their toll on the former priest. His once-black hair had turned almost completely gray. Wrinkles lined his forehead and circled his dark, deep-set eyes. Yet, there was a glow on his face that reflected the great transformation that had taken place in his heart. A reflection of God's infinite mercy and grace.

"Mama, Don Franco wants me to visit him in Milano." The smile on Nico's face stretched to both ears. "Is that not very kind of him?"

Maria's muscles tightened. "Most kind, indeed." Why did she feel threatened by Franco's invitation to Nico?

"Yes." Franco's voice was eager. "I would like very much for Nico to visit me. He would enjoy my students, and they would enjoy him." He turned toward Nico. "Moreover, it would give us an opportunity to get to know each other better."

A father longing to know his son. Of course. It was the most natural thing in the world. But was Maria ready for it? Hardly. Especially since she'd never told Nico the truth about Don Franco. That the former priest was his biological father.

Her heart raced. The awkwardness of the moment did not escape her. Eight years of living in America had distanced her from a past that still lived with her, embodied in her son Nico. And now, in his biological father who stood before her. Why had she not told Nico the truth about Franco? So many times she'd started to do so, but each time she'd stopped. Afraid. Tormented.

Ashamed.

Was it the fear of Nico's rejection? Of losing her son to his father? Of Franco's influence on Nico? At one time that might have been a problem, but Franco had truly repented. God's grace had transformed him into a Godly man who loved the

Lord with his whole heart. His influence on Nico would be nothing but good.

So, what was the resistance she felt at Franco's invitation to Nico?

"Maria! Maria Tonetta!" Maria instantly recognized the lilting voice. The same voice that had attempted to lure Luca— oh, so many years ago—into a marriage relationship.

Maria excused herself and approached the woman who'd desperately wanted to marry Maria's husband. "Teresa." Teresa stood before Maria, as beautiful and as radiant as ever. The years had done nothing to spoil the sparkle in her eyes, the lilt in her voice, nor the beauty of her figure.

"Ah, so you remember your old competitor, do you?" Teresa gave a laugh as she greeted Maria with a kiss on both cheeks.

Maria smiled. "I decided a long time ago to let bygones be bygones."

"Good advice. Besides, you won the coveted prize, not I."

Was there a tinge of regret in Teresa's voice?

Teresa embraced her. "How wonderful to see you after all these years! I'm sorry it has to be under these difficult circumstances."

Maria nodded. "I am so thankful Nico and I arrived in time to be with Mama during her final days."

"Indeed! It was a blessing. Living so far away can be a challenge when it comes to an emergency."

Teresa pointed toward Nico, standing by Franco a few paces away. "Is that your son? The little boy who was the talk of Pisano so many years ago?"

Maria flinched. Teresa still had the same old way of being flippant with her words. Why did those words still sting? Had Maria not put the horrendous rape behind her? Had she not been thankful for the treasured son Nico had become to her?

A son the deepest part of her did not want to lose.

Maria swallowed hard and forced a smile. "Yes, that's Nico." She called to him.

In an instant, Nico was at her side.

Maria took her son's arm. "Nico, do you remember Teresa Monastero, now Teresa Cosenza? She is an old friend of Papa. You were a little boy when she first met you."

Nico squinted, trying to remember. "I'm sorry. I guess I was too little of a lad to have paid attention." He extended a hand of greeting.

Teresa laughed. "I won't hold that against you." She gave Nico a hug. "The last time I saw you, you were just a little tyke." Teresa measured a child's height with her right hand. "I'm very sorry for your loss."

Nico nodded. "Thank you."

Teresa smiled and then turned to the young woman who had been standing quietly beside her. "I'd like you to meet my daughter, Sofia. You may not know that Sergio was a widower when I met him, and Sofia was four years old when her father and I married."

The girl was strikingly beautiful and shy. Long, dark tresses framed a face that was at once deep yet playful.

"Pleased to meet you, Sofia." Maria gently shook her hand.

"Likewise." Sofia's voice was angelic, as was her demeanor.

The girl's brown, dove-like eyes locked onto Nico's.

And Nico's locked onto hers.

A chill ran through Maria's veins. An unmistakable spark had ignited between the two young people.

Nico awkwardly extended his hand toward the young woman. She, in turn, graciously took it, lowering her eyes just slightly in the process, and then raising them again. They were aglow with the tenderness of budding attraction.

Maria's stomach knotted. She placed a hand on Nico's arm. "Nico, please go see if *Zio* Pietro needs your help carrying in more logs for the fire."

Nico gave Maria a bewildered look. "Very well, Mama." He left, but not without lingering his gaze for a brief moment on the face of the beautiful Sofia.

The boy was smitten. And that meant trouble.

Big trouble.

"A fine son you have there, Maria." Teresa's compliment seemed to add fuel to the fire raging in Maria's heart. Yes, Nico was, indeed, a fine son. The finest of all. But he was *her* son, and she would not allow him to become entangled with the daughter of the woman who once loved Maria's husband.

Teresa smiled, as though reading her thoughts. "So, how is Luca, my old beau?"

Maria bristled. Not only was the subject matter off limits, but to bring it up at Maria's mother's funeral was the height of impropriety. But when had Teresa ever been one to show sensitivity to the feelings of others?

Maria squared her jaw. "If I recall correctly, your relationship with Luca was one-sided."

Teresa raised her chin, her eyes narrowing. But she remained silent.

"He is doing well. I will tell him of your kindness in coming to Mama's funeral." Perhaps reminding Teresa of where she was would keep her insensitive comments in check.

"I am very glad to hear that. Please give him my warmest regards." She emphasized the word *warmest*.

Teresa turned to Sofia. "You never met Luca, but Nico's kind and gentle mannerisms remind me a lot of him—although Luca is not his birth father."

Maria's heart twisted. Did Teresa have to say that? Thank God Nico had left to help his uncle with the firewood. Who knew what more Teresa could have divulged about Nico's past? Maria must waste no time in telling him the whole truth.

Sofia raised a questioning eyebrow.

Teresa patted her daughter's arm. "No matter. I will explain everything to you later."

Maria would tell Nico the whole truth and tell him as soon as possible. Were Nico to discover the truth from anyone other than Maria herself, it would likely destroy their relationship forever. Or certainly damage it tremendously. Later that night, after the last guest left, she would take Nico aside and tell him the whole story about his birth. She must not delay any longer.

"Teresa, I would appreciate your not bringing up that topic, please. As you can understand, it is extremely sensitive." She would not reveal to Teresa that Nico himself did not yet know the truth.

Teresa's look conveyed remorse. "I'm sorry, Maria. It was rude of me to mention the matter. Please forgive me."

"I forgive you." Maria took a deep breath. "And now, if you will excuse me, I must check with Cristina to see if she needs my help in the kitchen. Thank you again for coming to pay your respects. It was most thoughtful of you." She kissed Teresa on both cheeks. Then, she turned to Sofia. "It was a pleasure to meet you, Sofia. You are a beautiful young woman. I'm sure your parents are very proud of you."

Sofia lowered her eyes and mumbled a thank you. "It was a pleasure to meet you, too, and"—she hesitated—"to meet your son."

Yes, my *son. And don't forget that he is my son!* Maria pushed aside the unkind thought. "Thank you."

With that, she left the room to find her sister.

Chapter Seven

His chest aching, Nico made his way down the long hallway to the kitchen and out to the backyard in search of *Zio* Pietro. Meeting Sofia had taken his breath away. Her dark, doe-shaped eyes had pierced his very soul like a bolt of lightning flashing through a stormy sky. Everywhere he turned, he saw those eyes. They drew him. Haunted him.

Mesmerized him.

They were at once innocent, yet alluring. Gentle, yet fiery. Kind, yet cruel.

His head spun as he tried to regain an emotional equilibrium that seemed lost to him forever. Like a tumbleweed driven by a powerful wind, his heart blew across the once-stable pathways of his reason, tossed in every direction by the unexpected dart of love-at-first-sight.

What was happening to him?

A half hour earlier, he'd been a rational and stable young man. After meeting Sofia, he'd turned into a jelly-kneed, blubbering fool obsessed with a young woman he'd just met.

It made no sense.

Yet, it made all the sense in the world.

Could it be he was in love? Or was it just infatuation?

He took in a deep breath. No. It had to be love. What else could turn his world into a violent tailspin in a moment's time? What else could make his insides tremble with a longing unlike anything he'd ever experienced?

What else could pierce his heart with such burning desire?

He was in love, and there was no turning back.

Never had a young woman struck him with the force with

which Sofia had struck him. His insides were a bundle of knots. His knees, limp.

His heart, aflame.

Was this what it meant to be in love?

How strange that Mama had sent him away to help *Zio* Pietro! And precisely at the moment when he'd wanted more than anything else to remain in Sofia's presence. Had Mama noticed his intense reaction upon meeting Sofia?

Something was going on, but Nico couldn't put his finger on it. All he knew was that he must see Sofia again. He must get to know her.

He must pursue a relationship with her.

He found *Zio* Pietro crossing the yard from the back shed to the veranda. His uncle chopped firewood from a grove of maple trees on the property and kept a steady supply of logs stacked on the back veranda. "*Zio*, let me help you."

"Thank you. I could use some help. Please go to the shed and grab another armload. That will give us enough wood to last the rest of the day and through the night."

Despite his suit attire in honor of *Nonna's* funeral, Nico proceeded to the back shed, picked up an armload of wood, carried it to the back veranda, and placed it carefully on the woodpile. Then he brushed off the pieces of bark from his suit vest and tie.

He turned to his uncle. "*Zio Pietro*, do you know Teresa Monastero from Ribera? Her married name is 'Cosenza.' Mama met her years ago, and she is here to pay her respects."

"I recall the name 'Monastero.' Her family used to live in Pisano, but after a tragic fire burned down their house during a violent storm, they moved to Ribera. Why do you ask?"

"Oh, I was just wondering." Dare he say anything to *Zio* Pietro about Sofia?

Zio Pietro put an arm around Nico's shoulder. "You've grown into a fine young man. I wish that you and your family would return to Sicily. It would be such a blessing to have you in our lives again."

"You know, *Zio*, I have been thinking about it. Seriously so. Ever since returning, I've had a longing to come home to my roots."

Zio Pietro winked at him. "There are lots of beautiful girls in the area who would love to have you as a husband. Most of the eligible young men have left for America, England, or other parts north." He chuckled. "If you return, I would have to protect you from the single young women." He broke into laughter. "I wouldn't want them stampeding you."

Nico smiled. He would share his heart with his uncle. "Thanks, *Zio*, but I think I've already found the girl I want."

Uncle Pietro raised an eyebrow. "Really? Who?"

Nico bit his lower lip. "May I tell you in confidence? Man to man?"

"Of course. Whatever you confide will stay between us."

Nico's heart swelled at his uncle's understanding. "I just met *Signora* Teresa's daughter, Sofia, and I think I've fallen in love with her."

Uncle Pietro slapped Nico on the back. "Well, I must say that's quick work for a young man who's been here only a few days."

"But, *Zio*, how does a man know when he's in love?"

A wistful look crossed *Zio* Pietro's face. He smiled and pointed to his heart. "One knows in here. In the depths of his heart."

"That's where I know it, *Zio*."

Zio Pietro looked Nico in the eye. "Pray, and let God work it out. If it is His will for you, it will come to pass."

Nico nodded. "Yes. I will pray. I want only God's will for my life." He smiled. "But I certainly hope it is God's will. It would be impossible to walk away from Sofia in my own strength. Only God could help me do that."

"Yes, you are right. But maybe you won't have to." He gave Nico a hug. "Now, let's go back to join the others. *Zia* Cristina is probably wondering what has happened to me." He laughed. "One thing a man does not want to incur is the wrath of a woman, especially when that woman is his wife."

Nico smiled. How blessed he was to have such an uncle! How wonderful it would be to live close by him and to learn from his wisdom!

As he followed Uncle Pietro back into the house, Nico prayed. *Lord, show me Your will. Show me if You want me to return to Sicily.*

Show me if you want me to marry Sofia.

As his spirit uttered the words, his heart echoed hope in response.

* * * *

Shaken by her recent conversation with Teresa, Maria found her middle sister Cristina alone in the kitchen, preparing another pot of espresso. The comforting aroma of the freshly brewing coffee reminded Maria of days gone by, when she and Mama would sit in this very kitchen, talking heart-to-heart over a cup of their favorite beverage. Maria's heart clenched.

Cristina stood by the stove, her reddened eyes revealing she'd been crying.

"Are you all right?" Maria approached her sister and embraced her.

Cristina sniffled and withdrew a white handkerchief from her pocket. "As well as can be expected under the circumstances, I guess." She dried her tears with the handkerchief.

Maria took her by the hand. "Here. Sit down with me for a moment."

Maria led her sister to the large, rectangular kitchen table. How many family meals she and her sisters had eaten as children around that table! In her mind's eye, she could still hear the joyous laughter. Still hear Papa's voice praying the prayer of thanksgiving before meals.

Still see Mama cooking at her iron stove.

A lump formed in Maria's throat. She swallowed hard and sat down in a chair beside her sister. "Has the house full of people been too much for you?"

Cristina shook her head. "No. Actually, the people have been a welcome distraction from the gnawing grief I'm feeling."

Gnawing described exactly how Maria was feeling, too. She took Cristina's hand and squeezed it. A keen regret for what she'd missed pierced Maria's heart. She resisted the temptation to envy the opportunity her two younger sisters had had to spend Mama's last years with her. Maria shook her head. No. She would not allow regret to consume her. Instead, she would be grateful she'd gotten to spend a few days with Mama before her death.

Cristina let go of Maria's hand. "Let me pour you some fresh coffee." Cristina rose and prepared a demitasse cup of espresso for each of them. "I'm thankful that so many relatives and friends have come from far and wide to pay their respects to Mama. She would have been encouraged. She was deeply loved, a shining example of what it means to love others."

Maria nodded, her heart overcome with a fresh wave of grief.

Cristina sighed. "When I came in here a few moments ago to make more coffee, I realized that not only is Mama gone, but *Bella Terra* will soon be gone as well. It will be the end of an era."

The blood in Maria's veins turned to ice. "What do you mean?"

Cristina's gaze locked onto Maria's. "You don't know?"

"Know what?" Maria's muscles tensed. "Obviously, I don't."

"We must sell *Bella Terra*." Cristina's voice trembled.

Maria's insides roiled. "But I knew nothing of this! When was it decided?"

"Actually, nothing has been officially decided yet. Luciana and I have been talking about it for the past several months, beginning at the onset of Mama's illness. I was sure I had alluded to it in a letter to you. If not, I'm deeply sorry. When Luciana attempted to broach the subject with Mama, she would hear nothing of it. Mama insisted that she would die here. She also made it clear that she didn't want us to sell the farm unless it was absolutely necessary. Unless we would go bankrupt by keeping it.

"Even then, however, she asked that we would explore every possible option before resorting to selling." Cristina lowered her eyes. "This place was her life. Just the thought of selling the farm pained her greatly." She raised her gaze toward Maria. "But we have no money left, my dear sister. It appears we have no choice but to put *Bella Terra* up for sale." Cristina took Maria's hand in hers. "Of course, Luciana and I planned to discuss the matter with you before you return to America. We are running out of funds and will have to make a decision soon."

The same fear of losing the family farm that Maria had felt years ago, after the rape. returned in full force. The same temptation to hopelessness.

The same challenge to her faith.

Fire rose in her belly. She'd saved the farm once; she'd save it again. "No! We can't sell *Bella Terra*! It's been in the family for almost two hundred years. It belongs to us. It belongs to our children as well. And to their children. It's the legacy we must leave them. Just as our ancestors left that legacy to us." She exhaled a long sigh. "I will not be remiss in passing the torch of that legacy. I will not be the one to break the chain of that legacy."

Cristina's eyes filled with tears. "I know, my dear sister.

You have always been the idealistic one. And I have always loved you for that. But financially I don't see any other choice. If we don't do something, we won't leave our children a legacy. We will leave them a bankruptcy."

Maria's mind went into survivor mode. "Was Mama aware of the seriousness of the situation?"

Cristina shook her head. "Frankly, I don't think so. Or else she chose to remain in denial. When she fell ill, we tried to keep the depressing details from her. She was suffering enough already without our adding to her distress. She knew the farm's financial situation was not good, but I don't think she knew how bad it really was."

Maria pondered Cristina's words. Her sisters had wanted to protect Mama. To keep her physical condition from worsening with added worries. Maria would have done the same thing.

Cristina wiped her eyes. "Mama never wanted to sell the farm. Despite our dire financial situation, we held out as long as we could in order to fulfill Mama's wish to die here. But now that she's gone, we can't endure much longer. The harvest has been meager for several years. We haven't earned enough from the sale of our produce to subsist on, let alone pay our help. We've had to dismiss all but two of the full-time farmhands. As for laborers, we hire them on a daily basis, as we need them. Pietro has been working the fields alongside the laborers for the last five years now. And Luciana and I have taken to working the fields ourselves. But now that I'm pregnant, I won't be able to continue for much longer. Only Roberto and Salvatore work for us fulltime now. And Salvatore works at half the pay he used to earn. We just didn't have the heart to let him go. Besides, at his age, no one would hire him."

Maria pictured old, faithful Salvatore. The dear, seventy-year-old man had been with the family ever since Maria was a little girl. He was more like an uncle to her than a farmhand.

He'd worked long, arduous days side by side with Maria's father. The two had been fast and loyal friends. Salvatore, his wife, and their children had attended family baptisms, anniversary parties, and religious celebrations with Papa, Mama, and their children. The relationship between the two families was close and loyal.

Cristina's voice interrupted Maria's thoughts. "Mama left the farm to the three of us. Even if we split the costs, we still wouldn't be able to sustain the expenses of continued, long-term upkeep."

"There has to be a way for us to keep *Bella Terra*. I'm sure of it."

"I wish I knew how." Cristina wrung her hands. "Your life is in America now. You have your own home to keep and your own expenses to pay in that country. Pietro and I have been living here and trying to earn a living from the land. But with the prolonged droughts we've had over recent years, the land has not yielded enough to sustain us longterm. Pietro has already begun to seek work elsewhere. As for Luciana, she plans to find work as a seamstress in a neighboring village."

Maria rose and walked to the large kitchen window overlooking the countryside. Outside, the setting sun cast long shadows over the purple-brown hillsides of *Bella Terra*. In the distance, the blue-green waters of the Mediterranean Sea sparkled like diamonds against the orange and crimson sky. Maria's soul stirred. Sicily might lack money, but it had no shortage of natural beauty. How she longed to return!

Her mind scrambled in a hundred different directions, searching for a way to prevent the sale of her beloved homestead. Short of a miracle, she and her sisters would be forced to sell the farm.

And to sell it soon.

She turned toward Cristina. "We'd better rejoin the others before our absence makes us seem discourteous."

"Yes. I agree."

Cristina rose.

Maria took her sister by the arm. "Let's talk about this more tomorrow."

Cristina nodded.

Every fiber of Maria's being rebelled against the thought of selling *Bella Terra*. She could not let it happen.

She would not let it happen.

To sell *Bella Terra* would mean reneging on the dream of four generations of Landros, a dream passed on to her father and then to her and her sisters. And to all of their children. Selling the farm would mean relinquishing a dream held, protected, and carried on for almost two hundred years by generations of Landros before her.

It would mean destroying a legacy.

No. She would not be the one to destroy the Landro legacy. She would not be the one to break the familial chain that had passed from generation to generation and that one day, she hoped, would pass to the next generation of Landros.

To Nico.

Her heart lurched. What was she thinking? Nico was an illegitimate son. A *bastardo*, as the villagers had called him. Bearing no legal right to an inheritance. No legal right to *Bella Terra*.

No legal right to anything that was hers.

Only Anna and Valeria, as well as her sisters' children, had a legal right to inherit the family farm.

She pushed aside the heart-wrenching truth.

As they left the kitchen, Cristina spoke. "Tomorrow, I will fetch Luciana, and then the three of us can discuss what to do about the farm."

Maria nodded. "Very well."

Yes, she and her two sisters would make a final decision. But Maria had already made hers. Her vote regarding the sale of *Bella Terra* would be a resounding "No!"

Chapter Eight

Shortly after the last guest left, Maria climbed the stairway to her old bedroom. She needed time to sort out the unrest boiling within her after the happenings of the afternoon. Her conversation with Cristina about the sale of *Bella Terra* had left her stomach in knots and her heart in shreds.

She lay down on her old bed and stared at the cream-colored ornate ceiling. Swirls of stucco formed a design that reminded her of clouds on a hot summer afternoon. As a child, she would imagine all kinds of animal figures in those swirls. She would even picture herself sitting on the edge of one of the imaginary clouds, dangling her legs over her bed below.

She took a deep breath. What good days they had been! The days of childhood. Carefree. Timeless.

Full of limitless possibilities.

She drew her thoughts back to the present. To the pressing matter at hand. Both Cristina and Luciana felt they had to sell the farm. And so did Pietro. Not that he had any legal say in the matter. But keeping the farm would be a financial burden on him as Cristina's husband. Maria couldn't blame him for his opinion.

Nor could she blame her sisters. After all, they had been the ones to carry the brunt of the expenses. Maria and Luca had barely been able to meet their own expenses in Brooklyn and, much to her regret, had not sent a penny to help pay the expenses of *Bella Terra*. The original plan had been that they would send money every month from America. But that plan had backfired, and backfired badly. What could one do when one had no money to send? If they'd remained in Sicily, she,

Luca, and the children could have at least worked the fields. She could have at least sold the little produce they harvested to the surrounding villages.

She could have done something.

She wrapped her arms tightly around her chest, fighting off the temptation to indulge her regret. Hindsight was always better than foresight. But looking back did not solve any problems. It only created new ones.

And worse ones.

No wonder the Lord admonished His followers to forget those things that lay behind and to press forward toward those things that lay ahead.

And then there was Franco's invitation to Nico. Her son's interest in getting to know his birth father troubled her. Deeply. More than she was willing to admit. Yet, what right did she have to squelch it? None whatsoever. Nico was a grown man now. If he wanted to establish a relationship with his birth father, he had every right to do so. Were she to attempt to stop him, she would only fan her son's desire to reconnect with Franco. To explore his roots on Franco's side.

She sighed. The whole situation ate at her. Stirred up emotions she'd thought long buried. Envy. Resentment.

Fear.

She rubbed her hand across her forehead. What was happening to her? Where did these negative feelings come from? And why were they surfacing now? Hadn't she overcome all of the negative emotions associated with the rape? Hadn't she forgiven Franco and the townspeople who'd scorned her and shunned her?

Hadn't she put the past behind her once and for all? Was she destined to revisit over and over again the greatest pain of her life for the rest of her life?

And, finally, there was her earlier distressing conversation with Teresa. Maria's stomach clenched. The woman was still in love with Luca. Or so it seemed. Why else would she mention her former interest in Maria's husband? And what gall to mention it at Mama's funeral!

Maria swallowed the bile that rose to her throat. Wasn't it enough that she was dealing with overwhelming grief from Mama's death? Did she now have to deal with Teresa's unwelcome intrusion into a past that Maria had long ago put behind her? Would that past forever return to haunt her?

As if the problems with *Bella Terra*, Franco, and Teresa weren't enough, Nico was smitten with Sofia. It was so obvious the girl had touched that deepest place in his heart where love is ignited and where love blooms. Maria knew her son. She knew his pure and tender heart. His guilelessness.

His vulnerability.

The thought of Nico's marrying Teresa's daughter was more than Maria could bear. It would mean re-establishing a connection between Teresa and Luca through the marriage of their children.

It would mean that she and Teresa would be grandmothers to the same grandchildren.

The hair on the nape of Maria's neck bristled.

No! She could not have it. She would not have it. She would not allow Nico to marry Sofia. She would not lose her son to the daughter of the woman who might still harbor feelings for Luca.

To the woman who'd been a thorn in Maria's side from the moment she'd met her.

To the woman who knew of her past in a way that threatened Maria's peace.

Maria's body shook all over. She sat up in her old bed. The bed she'd slept in as a child. The bed she and Luca had shared as husband and wife before leaving Sicily for America.

She looked around. Her old bedroom looked the same. Just as she'd left it years earlier. Only the wallpaper on one wall had faded, the place where the sun shone upon it each morning. How she'd loved greeting the new day upon awakening in this room every morning as a child! The memory of the aroma of freshly baked bread and homemade sausage frying in the kitchen below where Mama prepared breakfast brought sudden tears to her eyes.

Then open, wrenching sobs.

A wave of unbearable grief swept over her. Back and forth Maria rocked, clutching her sides, while torrents of hot, stinging tears poured from her eyes. Her soul.

Her heart.

A heart that broke into a million pieces as the realization struck her that Mama was gone. The woman who had borne her. Nurtured her. Stood by her when she was pregnant out of wedlock. Helped her raise her illegitimate son. The woman who had been a bedrock of unconditional love, a bastion of strength after Maria's papa died.

A beacon of hope when all seemed lost.

Mama was really gone. Gone forever.

Until this moment, the truth had not fully struck Maria. But now, it hit her with soul-shattering force. How she wished Luca were here to comfort her!

She threw herself on the bed and wept bitterly for several long moments. Until there were no more tears left inside her. Only numbness.

By the time she rose from the bed, night had fallen over *Bella Terra*. A full moon shone through the white lace curtains, casting a broad swath of light over the worn, oaken floor.

Maria rose from the bed and walked to the water basin. She cupped her hands, filled them with water, and then splashed it onto her reddened eyes. Taking the hand towel by the basin, she wiped her eyes dry.

It was time to find Nico.

To tell him the truth about his parentage before someone else did.

She made her way to the kitchen.

Cristina was cleaning up the last of the dishes. "Ah, there you are!" her sister gently reprimanded. "I have been looking for you."

"I was upstairs in my old bedroom."

"Crying."

"Yes, crying."

"I can tell. Your eyes are swollen and crimson red."

Maria's eyes filled again with tears. "The truth of Mama's death is just starting to hit me. The pain of losing her is overwhelming."

Cristina gave her a tight hug. "I understand. It must be more difficult for you since you've been away. I've been here, watching her die, preparing myself emotionally for the moment when she would leave us for a better place. For you, it was a sudden shock. For me, it has been a gradual adjustment to an inevitable end."

Maria squeezed her sister to her heart. "I feel so guilty about having left Sicily."

"You did nothing wrong. You followed your husband. That was the right and godly thing to do."

"I know. But why, then, do I feel so guilty?"

"Because you loved Mama. And perhaps because you feel that your leaving her brought on her illness."

Cristina had a matter-of-fact way of getting to the core of a problem. To those underlying reasons that are often hidden and unsuspected.

"Besides," her sister continued, "grief robs us of our capacity to think straight. It causes our emotions to take the place of reason. And we always get into trouble when we do that." Cristina smiled. "So, don't dwell on the past and on your feelings of guilt. Think about the future and the blessings that lie ahead." Cristina paused. "Most of all, live in the present. That's what Mama would have wanted you to do."

Live in the present. Why did Maria always have such a hard time doing that? Her life was a constant tension between the past and the future, the future and the past. The present had little place in her life.

Yet, truth be told, the present was life. All she had was the present. The past was gone forever. The future was promised to no one. But the present was God's gift to her now.

The Now. God was the God of the Now. If she wanted to experience Him, she must live in the Now. In God, there was no Past. No Future.

Only Now.

And in eternity, there would be only Now.

Maria took in a deep breath. "You are right. Mama always lived in the present. She knew how to savor every moment. She didn't fret about the past. She hoped the best for the future. But she lived—really lived—in the present."

Cristina nodded. "When we live in the present, we are freed from worry. Our God lives outside of time. And time is subject to Him. Therefore, the past and the future as we know it are both in His hands. As is the present."

Maria smiled. "You would have made a great philosopher."

Cristina chuckled. "Pietro says that, too.

"Did I hear you mention my name?" Pietro came through the back door into the kitchen.

Cristina laughed. "Yes, I was telling Maria that, like her, you think I would have made a good philosopher."

Pietro put his arm around Cristina and hugged her close. "I do. And it's my job to keep you grounded." He planted a kiss on her cheek.

A sudden yearning for Luca filled Maria's heart. "It seems to be the same with Luca and me. He keeps me grounded as well."

Pietro chuckled. "I think God deliberately connects two opposites so they will balance each other."

Maria nodded and smiled. "I'm thinking, however, of asking Luca if he would like to philosophize with me for once and consider moving back to Sicily."

Cristina raised an eyebrow. "Are you sure about this, Maria? Or are you simply feeling the need to be around family at this difficult time?"

"I think a little bit of both."

"Of course, we would love to have you return. But do you think Luca would agree?"

"Honestly, I don't know. He still thinks God has called us to America. He still thinks we can succeed much better in America than in Sicily."

"How have you fared since you've been there?"

Maria looked into her sister's kind eyes. "Truth be told, it has been very difficult. Far more difficult than either one of us ever expected. Our lives consist of work, work, work, with a little play thrown in now and then. The only friends we've made are people in the Italian community, most of whom are in the same position as we are. Of course, we have our church family as well. As I've mentioned in my letters to you, the climate is very cold in the winter, and the city air is contaminated with industrial smoke." She sighed. "I don't mean to complain, but I miss the clear blue skies and the vast open spaces of *Bella Terra*."

Pietro spoke. "Luca is a man who hears the voice of God. If God is calling you to return to your homeland, then Luca will know."

Cristina patted Maria's hand. "Let's pray for God's will to be done. If He wants you to move back, He will speak to Luca's heart."

"Yes, you are right. May God's will be done." Maria secretly hoped God's will would be her will, too. She needed to be back with her family. She needed to be back in Sicily.

She needed to return to *Bella Terra*.

Just then Nico entered the kitchen. "Mama, I have been looking for you. Don Franco has invited me to leave for Milano with him tomorrow morning."

Maria's insides jolted. "That is sooner than I thought. Before you leave, I must speak with you. It's quite urgent and cannot wait any longer."

Nico's face paled. "What is it, Mama?"

"Come with me." Maria excused herself from Cristina and Pietro and motioned to Nico to follow her.

Her heart pounding, she climbed the staircase to his childhood bedroom and, once he had entered behind her, she securely closed the door.

As she sat down in the old rocking chair by the window— the one in which she'd rocked him as a baby— she whispered a desperate prayer for wisdom.

* * * *

Nico sat cross-legged on his old bed while Mama rocked slowly in the rocking chair. His heart beat with the rush of a thousand stampeding stallions. What news could be so urgent that Mama would have to tell him on the day of *Nonna's* funeral? Was it related to *Nonna*? To *Bella Terra*?

To the farm's financial collapse?

One frightening question after another bombarded his racing mind.

He waited patiently, his stomach roiling.

Mama folded her hands in her lap. Her face looked pale; her gaze, troubled. Tension lines framed her eyes and her mouth.

She drew in a deep breath. "Nico, what I must tell you is something I should have told you many years ago. For that, I ask you to forgive me." She hesitated, her lower lip quivering. "It involves Don Franco. I want you to know this before you leave with him for Milano tomorrow morning." Her voice hitched.

"And before anyone else tells you." She lowered her gaze.

Nico's stomach muscles tied themselves into a dozen knots. Was Mama about to confirm the thoughts he'd had about Don Franco? He riveted his full attention on his mother, his blood pounding against the walls of his veins.

Mama stopped rocking. Her gaze locked onto his.

Nico held his breath.

"When I was a young girl of seventeen, I was engaged to be married to a young man from Pisano named Carlo Mancini. Carlo was a year older than I. We'd grown up together and were very much in love.

In order to earn some money for our wedding and our future life together, I took a job at the parish rectory in Pisano. At the time, Don Franco was the head pastor, assisted by Don Vincenzo. Don Franco had also been my teacher during my years in the only school in Pisano." Mama paused and took another deep breath. "Back then, Don Franco was a strange man. He always made me feel uncomfortable because of the lustful way he looked at me, but I tried not to think about it. Instead, I focused on my studies and avoided him as much as possible."

Nico listened intently. Question after bewildering question assailed his mind, making it reel with uncertainty. He wanted desperately to interrupt Mama for answers, but he kept silent, reluctant to interrupt her train of thought.

Mama lifted her gaze and sighed. "I told Carlo about my discomfort around Don Franco, but Carlo said I was imagining it. After all, Franco was a priest, and a priest was a holy man." Mama lowered her eyes. "But I felt differently." She wrung her hands. "When I took the job at the rectory, I was assigned to work with Rosa, the priests' cook and the one in charge of overseeing the care and maintenance of the rectory. Rosa took me under her wing and became like a second mother to me."

Nico's heart raced while he did his best to follow Mama's somewhat erratic story.

Part of him wanted to hear everything she had to say; another part of him dreaded hearing something that could change his life forever.

Mama lowered her voice. "One day I went to work as usual only to discover that Rosa was out sick for the day and Don Vincenzo was away on business. Don Franco and I were alone in the rectory."

A cold, black sensation rushed into the pit of Nico's stomach, turning it to ice. He began to shake. Where was his mother going with this? How could he avoid hearing more?

Could he stop her?

But hear more he must. He must know the full truth, no matter how ugly that truth was. He must listen to every word Mama spoke because, on a very deep level, his very identity depended on it.

She continued, her voice at once sad, yet deliberate. "I thought I should go home for the day, but Don Franco insisted I stay. He said he would be working in his office and would not disturb me. I could go about my business as usual and then leave when I finished."

Mama paused for a long moment, her eyes fixed on a distant memory that still deeply affected her life. "Against my better judgment, I remained and, as was my daily custom, I went upstairs to the second floor to clean the priests' sleeping quarters. While I was cleaning Don Franco's room, he suddenly entered to retrieve some papers he said he'd left on his dresser. His sudden appearance startled me. But what startled me even more was the crazed look in his eyes. For all of his strangeness, I'd never seen that look before. It was maniacal. Diabolic.

"Ominous.

"My heart trembled. I started to leave the room, but he told me he would not be long. Only a moment to retrieve his papers.

"I waited patiently for him to finish, all the while wondering if I should run out of the room. Yet, I was afraid to do so.

"He walked toward his dresser, gathered his papers, and then turned toward me.

"His eyes were glazed over and far away, like those of a madman.

"My blood turned to ice.

"In his hand, between his thumb and his index finger, he held a gold wedding band. He said he'd purchased it for the girl he'd planned to marry before entering the priesthood. He then told me he wanted to give the ring to me.

"I broke out in a cold sweat. Horrified at his offer, I refused the ring and then ran toward the door. In a fit of rage, he grabbed me by the arm and threw me on the bed."

Mama lowered her eyes. "And raped me." Her words came in an anguished whisper.

Like the battering winds of a cyclone, Mama's words shook Nico's soul. "And I am the product of that rape." His voice was a hoarse whisper.

Mama nodded, tears spilling down her cheeks. "When Carlo learned of it, he abandoned me."

Nico's soul shattered as the shrapnel from Mama's words embedded itself deep within his heart. He'd suspected he was Franco's son, but he'd never suspected that his mother had been raped.

Why had she hidden this from him all of these years? Did she fear his reprisal? His retribution?

His rejection?

Nico's insides twisted like a snake slithering along the ground in search of prey. Could he ever trust his mother again? If she'd kept his paternity hidden from him, what else had she kept hidden from him? And Papa? He'd been complicit in maintaining silence. Could he ever trust Papa again?

Nico rose from the bed and walked over to the casement window, his stomach tied into a tight knot. Below, the hillsides of *Bella Terra* undulated downward toward Pisano, merging into the lowlands that then extended to the Mediterranean Sea.

One burning question tormented his mind. Who was he? Who really was he? He was the adopted son of Luca Tonetta who had raised him. He was also the biological son of a man whom he'd grown to respect years ago as his teacher and as foreman at *Bella Terra*, but never as a father. Would he ever respect him again?

Could he?

And should he still go to Milano with the man who'd raped his mother, even if that man was his father?

Mama's quiet weeping drew Nico's attention away from himself. He turned from the window and walked over to her, part of him boiling with anger, another part of him filled with compassion.

Torn inside by conflicting emotions, he fell to one knee beside her and placed a hand on her arm. "Mama, why didn't you tell me sooner?" His voice broke. "Why didn't you tell me Don Franco was my father?"

Her tear-filled gaze lifted toward him. "Luca is your true father. He is the one who raised you as his own son."

Nico's heart sank. Mama didn't understand. Yes, Luca had raised him. Provided for him.

Cared for him.

But Nico wasn't connected to Luca in the same way he was connected to Franco. Nor would he ever be. He was linked to Franco through a bloodline that had formed Nico's very identity. His very physical traits.

His very soul.

As much as Luca loved him, Luca could never give him what Nico longed for most—a link to a history. To a past that stretched far back in time.

To a past that was uniquely his.

Nico buried his head in Mama's lap. His body shook, but

his heart shook even more. His life would never be the same.

Never!

Yet, a spark of hope rose within him. He would have a few days with Don Franco to learn of his true roots. Perhaps Franco's invitation was a blessing in disguise. Perhaps it was God's way of answering the cry of Nico's heart to know who he truly was.

In a few short hours, his emotions had plummeted from the heights of ecstasy at meeting Sofia to the depths of despair at learning the truth about the rape. Tears welled up in his eyes. He lifted his head and looked at Mama. "What am I to do now, Mama? I have already accepted Don Franco's invitation to go with him to Milano, but I no longer want to go."

"You must go."

"But this news has colored my view of him."

"Nico, you must forgive him. I know it is difficult, but our Lord commands it."

"Have you forgiven him, Mama?"

Maria nodded. "I forgave him many years ago. Forgiving him set me free."

"Then I will forgive him, too."

"Don Franco eventually came to Christ and is now a new creation in Him. Old things have passed away. All things have become new."

Nico pondered the familiar Scripture verse in 2 Corinthians 5:17. It clearly stated that when one accepts Christ as Savior and Lord, one becomes a new creation. Don Franco was a new creation. He was no longer a lustful criminal guilty of rape. He'd been washed clean by the blood of Christ and now stood pure before Him.

Nico looked into Mama's anguished eyes. He must forgive her as well for keeping the truth from him. "Mama, I must forgive you, too. I confess that your hiding the truth from me for so long has angered me to the point of tempting me to lose trust in you. But I want to see the situation from your perspective. I am deeply sorry you endured such horrible suffering."

Mama cupped his face with her hands. "You were worth every bit of the suffering, my son. Oh, so very worth it!" She placed a kiss on his forehead.

A lump formed in Nico's throat.

Mama stroked his chin. "When we love the Lord, He works everything out for our ultimate good."

But would God's promise hold true regarding Sofia? When Sofia discovered Nico was an illegitimate son, would God work out his relationship with her for Nico's ultimate good? Or would Sofia reject him forever?

Chapter Nine

The next day, Maria sat down with Cristina and Luciana at the kitchen table to discuss the sale of *Bella Terra*. The house was still, except for the incessant pecking of a woodpecker outside the kitchen window. A votive candle sat on the kitchen table, casting flickering shadows on the white linen tablecloth. Beside it stood a small ceramic vase filled with white Shasta daisies left over from Mama's funeral service.

Maria's soul ached at the prospect of reading Mama's will. It served as a heart-wrenching reminder that Mama was truly dead. Gone forever. That reality struck Maria with full force in the pit of her stomach, trying to knock the wind out of a place where there was no more wind. If only she could turn back the clock. If only she could relive the last eight years.

If only she could rewrite her past.

A painful lump formed in her throat. There was nothing to do but move forward. Finish out her days on this earth as Mama had finished hers. One day she and Mama would be reunited in Heaven, never more to part. She drew in a deep breath. This was the hope of all those who knew Jesus Christ and believed in the resurrection of the body. She should rejoice because Mama's suffering was over.

Despite the fact that her own had just begun.

Not that she'd never experienced grief. When Papa died, her heart had broken. He'd been her hero. Her mentor.

Her protector.

When she'd lost her innocence by rape, she'd experienced the tortuous grief of a violation so abominable that nothing could compare with it.

But losing Mama had brought a different kind of grief. A primal grief that reached into the deepest places of connection between mother and child. A place where the heart remained silent simply because it could not speak.

Cristina led the conversation. "I know this is difficult for all of us, but it is something we must do to fulfill Mama's wishes. Shortly before she died, Mama drew up a will and instructed us to read it after her funeral. So, here we are."

With trembling hands, Cristina withdrew Mama's will from the large white envelope in which it had been placed and spread it out on the table before them. The will was short—only two pages in length. In those two pages lay Mama's wishes for *Bella Terra* and her daughters' futures.

Maria followed along as Cristina read the words. "The Last Will and Testament of Concetta Landro." Maria swallowed hard and continued reading, following along with Cristina. "I bequeath to my three daughters—Maria, Cristina, and Luciana—the entire estate of *Bella Terra* to be divided equally among them. It is my express desire that the estate remain in the possession of my daughters, if possible. But, if not possible, then I leave to my three daughters the decision in common as to what to do with the property."

So Mama was aware of the financial challenges the farm faced. How could she not have been? Had she not run the farm since Papa's death? Surely she knew the farm was losing money. But, perhaps, she was as much of an idealist as Maria was.

Maria continued reading silently while Cristina read aloud. "My prayer is that my daughters will seek God's will in the matter of the estate. That they would not allow fear or doubt to dictate their decision, but that they would allow the peace of God to arbitrate every choice."

Maria interrupted Cristina's reading. "Notice that Mama directed us to pray first, to seek God's will in all decisions we make. Let's pray now."

Taking hold of her sisters' hands, Maria led them in a fervent prayer for God's wisdom in their every decision regarding *Bella Terra*.

"Amen," the three sisters proclaimed in unison.

Luciana raised an index finger. "According to Mama's will, all three of us must decide together on whether to keep the farm or to sell it."

Cristina nodded. "Yes, that is the first order of business. And, it seems to me, the most important."

Maria's muscles tensed. "It's no secret that I do not want to sell the farm. I know you both disagree, but there's something in me that vehemently resists the idea. I just don't feel right about it."

Luciana's voice was gentle but urgent. "We don't want to sell *Bella Terra*, either, dear sister. But we have no choice. Unless you can show us a way to keep the farm, we will not be able to sustain the expenses. We have been losing money for a long time, and our creditors have been knocking at our door. We can't go on like this much longer before falling into bankruptcy."

Maria rose and began to pace the kitchen floor. "There has to be a way to save *Bella Terra*. There simply has to be." She released a long breath. "Mama always used to say that if there is a will, there is a way."

Cristina sighed. "I guess the crucial question then is, "Do we have the will to keep *Bella Terra* in our possession?'"

Maria stopped short, Cristina's question provoking her to anger. "Well, do we?"

Luciana, ever the level-headed one, intervened. "We may have the will, but do we have the means? A will to do something is nothing without the means to do it."

Maria's voice rose slightly. "But the will creates the means, not the other way around! Don't you see?"

Luciana smiled. "Maria, you've always been the idealist

among us. And I suppose idealists see beyond what realists see." She leaned back in her chair. "Please. Don't get me wrong. Idealism is a wonderful thing. But there are times when we must put idealism aside and embrace realism and practicality."

Maria stood firm. "I don't know if it's a matter of being an idealist, although I certainly am one. It's a matter of whether or not we want to preserve a family legacy of almost two hundred years or surrender it to circumstances that seem beyond our control but are not. I, for one, say let's fight for what is ours. Our parents, grandparents, great-grandparents, and our ancestors of several generations before them paid a great price to build, establish, and maintain *Bella Terra*. We would be dishonoring their memory if we sell the fruit of their hard work."

Cristina leaned back in her chair. "I think all of us want to preserve the family legacy, Maria. But wanting to and being able to are two different things." She looked at Maria, her facial expression revealing a growing frustration with her older sister. "Sometimes we have to let go of a dream in order to survive."

Maria's soul screamed *No*! She would never let go of a dream in order to survive. Especially the dream of preserving her family's legacy. Surviving wasn't living. Surviving was merely existing. And one would be better off dead than merely surviving or existing. The difference between living and existing was the difference between life and death.

She fought back the temptation to despair. "We are dealing with two issues here. One is the decision to sell or not to sell and the other is the set of problems we will face as a result of either decision." She waved a hand in the air. "The first question we have to decide among ourselves is whether or not we will sell the farm. After that question has been answered— and only then—should we decide how to handle the problems that will arise as the result of that particular decision—whatever that decision may be. Does that make sense?"

"Yes, it makes sense." Luciana agreed. "But my way of thinking is that we should first determine the results we want and then make the decision that will get us those results."

Maria had to admit that Luciana's suggestion made sense, too. "All right, then. What results do you want?"

Cristina jumped in. "We want to be free of a financial burden that is weighing us down, crushing us, robbing us of the joy of life. A burden that threatens to destroy us financially, possibly for the rest of our lives." She rubbed her hand across her forehead. "I agree with Luciana. Since Pietro and I married, we have not earned enough income from the farm to support us. Nor has there been enough to support Luciana. She plans to take a job as a seamstress. Pietro is looking for work as well, which leaves us with two fewer people to work the farm."

Maria's heart clenched. Her sister's argument was valid. Maria had not witnessed firsthand the burden the farm had been for her family. Was she being unfair to ask them to do something for which only they would suffer, while she herself returned to America?

Yet, why did her heart so vehemently oppose selling the farm?

"Would you consider the possibility that keeping the farm might work after all?"

"I don't see how that is a possibility." Cristina's voice sounded irritated. "Selling the farm will eliminate the financial problem, while keeping the farm will not. It seems pretty simple and straightforward to me."

"But what about the problems that will ensue if we sell?" Maria's question hung in mid-air.

Cristina turned toward her and sighed. "What problems? I don't see any problems at all that will result from selling the farm. I see only benefits."

Maria composed herself. "Well, consider the problem of remorse and regret. The sorrow at losing a legacy that has been handed down to us for almost two hundred years through several generations by our faithful ancestors who held on to the legacy and the dream. What would they think of us for abandoning both and relinquishing the torch to strangers?" Maria shuddered as her impassioned voice rose even higher. "The loss of a rich, two-hundred-year-old heritage and legacy preserved and passed down to us through four generations and through much sacrifice." She faced both of her sisters. "Do you not think we will be plagued with regret if we sell? Frankly, I would be embarrassed to face our ancestors were I to meet them on the street."

Luciana chuckled. "But you know that won't happen, Maria. They're dead."

Although she'd meant it in jest, Luciana's comment annoyed Maria. She pressed her point. "Then there's the problem that selling will create a host of other problems. For instance, what if the buyer doesn't take care of the property or turns it into something other than a home—like a restaurant or a hotel or a—." Maria paused mid-sentence as a light suddenly went on in her brain. Her heart soared. "Now that might be a way to save *Bella Terra!*"

"What do you mean?" Luciana's gaze locked onto hers.

"I mean we could turn the farm into an inn or a hotel. Or even a restaurant. Or both."

Cristina rolled her eyes.

Luciana's eyes widened in surprise. "Are you serious?"

"Yes. I am very serious. In fact, I couldn't be more serious."

"But who would run it?" Cristina rubbed her forehead. "And who would come here to stay at our hotel? We are not on the main road to anywhere. And our economy is so impoverished that people don't have money to feed their families, let alone stay in quaint hotels."

Dismissing Cristina's objections, Maria grew more and

more excited. "Still, there are people from other countries who travel. People from England and America. People from Germany and Holland. Not every country is as impoverished as Sicily. In fact, turning *Bella Terra* into an inn or a hotel could actually help not only make us money but also boost our local economy." Maria paused. "Yes, it would be tough at first, and all of us would certainly have to make sacrifices. But once we started turning a profit, we could—"

"We could what, Maria?" Cristina broke in, her voice weary. "Remember. You live in America." A touch of sarcasm edged her voice. "And what if we didn't start turning a profit? What if we lost even more money?"

"Why do you always look on the negative side? Can't you see the possibilities?"

Cristina shook her head.

Luciana looked thoughtful. "You know, Maria. You might be on to something."

At least one of her sisters was open-minded. Two out of three would make a majority and enable them to keep the farm.

But Cristina still held back. "Turning *Bella Terra* into an inn would require thousands of *lire* for repairs and renovations. Before we could get it into decent enough shape for business, we would have to expend a lot of money repairing, renovating, and restoring. Where would we get the money to do that?"

Maria squared her jaw. "We could take out a loan and then repay it with the profit earned from the hotel."

Luciana looked concerned. "We would have to use the farm as collateral. And if we don't earn enough profit to repay the loan, we would lose the farm altogether, with nothing to show for it. It would be as bad as giving it away outright."

Maria pondered her sister's words. Luciana was a sensible woman, and her words made sense in light of their grave financial need.

But, still, Maria could not let go of the dream. She drew in a deep breath.

"Would you at least consider the possibility?"

Cristina's face grew pensive. "Maria, do you think you might be thinking only of yourself? Of your own desires for *Bella Terra*, and not of our common future?"

Cristina's words were a blow to Maria's stomach, not to mention her ego. "How could you even think such a thing of me?" Yet, her sister's words made her examine her heart. Was she indeed being selfish? Was she thinking only of herself? Did her desire to keep the farm stem from a need to hold on to the past? A past that she would do better to let go? Was this the real reason she could not—would not—give in to the idea of selling *Bella Terra*?

Luciana's gentle voice interrupted Maria's thoughts. "We could argue back and forth all night, my dear sisters. In my opinion, the most important thing for us to do is to determine the Lord's will on the matter." Her gaze moved from Maria to Cristina and back again. "What do you think God wants us to do?"

A pause ensued. Then Maria spoke. "I've given you my thoughts. I think God wants us to keep the farm."

Luciana turned to their other sister. "And you, Cristina?"

"I think we should aim for a unanimous decision. That, in my opinion, would please Mama the most."

"True." Luciana leaned forward on her elbows. "But, what if we can't reach a unanimous decision?"

"Then we will have to go with a simple majority." Cristina sighed. "My vote is to sell."

Maria took her seat again. "Cristina, think of this. Do you not wish to pass on our family inheritance to our children? Would we not be depriving them of their rightful heritage?"

Cristina objected. "Maria, I love the farm as much as you do. But you've been living in America for the past several years. You don't know the difficulty of keeping this place running." Cristina sighed. "Besides, with the new baby coming, Pietro and I will have even less time to run an inn."

"Suppose we divide our duties. If Luca and I move back, the work would not be too much for any one of us. As for running the establishment, we could all pitch in." She pointed to Cristina. "You could be the cook. Just think. Our guests would enjoy the fruit of your amazing culinary skills."

Then Maria turned to her youngest sister. "Luciana, you could be the chief administrator. You have a gift for organization. For knowing what to do first and what to do next. You would be a natural in this position."

Maria's pulse raced as the dream grew in her mind and heart. "And I—well, I could oversee the food supply. I have lots of experience doing that, and I love being out in the fields."

Cristina repeated her earlier objection. "But you live in America."

Yes. Living in America was a major obstacle. But only for the time being. Once back in Brooklyn, she would do her best to convince Luca to return to Sicily. "Yes, we do live in America, but perhaps not for much longer."

Her sisters raised their eyebrows.

"I was serious when I said I plan to ask Luca to move us back to Sicily."

"Would Luca even consider moving back? And moving back to help run an inn? He is a tailor by trade, after all."

Cristina asked a valid question.

"Honestly, I don't know. But it's worth asking him. We certainly haven't met with great financial success in Brooklyn. It might be time to return to Sicily."

Maria walked to the window and stood there for a long moment. Although she'd present her idea to Luca, was she truly convinced he'd agree? Knowing her husband as she did, he'd likely object to her idea and declare it a closed matter. Yet, Luca was not unreasonable. If she showed him the advantages of moving back, he might agree.

Maria turned away from the window and faced her sisters. "I will ask Luca when I return to Brooklyn."

But, truth be told, doubt assailed her heart. To ask Luca to return to Sicily would be asking him to give up his dream. But what if she could convince him that his dream had little, if any, hope of fulfillment in America? What if she could show him that returning to Sicily was in their best interests and in the interests of their children?

Luciana placed her elbows on the table and leaned forward. "Suppose you do convince Luca to return. That still doesn't solve our problem. We are facing a collapsed economy. Unless the farm can generate income for us, it is a lost cause."

Maria jumped in. "Nothing is a lost cause. We just have to find a way to make it work. And the idea of turning *Bella Terra* into a hotel and restaurant just might be that way."

Cristina spoke up. "Frankly, Maria, I think you're being unrealistic. Pietro, Luciana, and I have been trying to make *Bella Terra* work ever since you left. We've poured our hearts and souls into preserving the farm, but we've met with nothing but financial losses on every side. We have no control over drought nor over the Sicilian economy. Even most of our wells have run dry, prohibiting the watering of crops. No business-person in his right mind would continue operating at a loss year after year as we have done for a long time. We did it for Mama's sake. But we cannot go on like this. It would be insanity. It would take nothing less than a miracle of God to keep *Bella Terra* in the family."

Maria placed her hands on the table and leaned on it. "Well, God is in the miracle business, isn't He?"

Cristina looked up at her. "I will never say God doesn't perform miracles, but if God saves *Bella Terra*, then that will rank right up there with parting the Red Sea."

Maria smiled. "So, why not give Him a chance to prove Himself to us?"

But even as she spoke the question, she wondered if she were tempting God.

Cristina shook her head. "I think it's too late for miracles. Both Luciana and I feel the need to sell." She turned toward Luciana. "Right, Luciana?"

Luciana nodded. "I think that is the best course of action, even though I liked your idea about an inn, Maria. Frankly, though, I don't think it is financially feasible."

Cristina turned back to Maria. "That's two of us in favor of selling and one of us opposed. I think the majority vote should settle the issue."

Maria's heart sank. She looked at Luciana. "So, that is your final decision?"

Luciana nodded. "I'm sorry, Maria."

Darkness fell on Maria's soul. Mama didn't say in her will that the decision had to be unanimous. She'd said only that the decision had to be shared. They had complied with Mama's wishes. They had respected her will.

There was nothing more Maria could do.

Or was there?

* * * *

Nico sat across from his birth father in the latter's modest apartment on the grounds of Milano's prestigious Classical Academy for Boys. A single Tiffany lamp graced a small mahogany table to the side of Nico's chair and lit the sparsely furnished living area where Franco made his abode. In the large stone fireplace, a blazing fire crackled warmth into the room as its bright flames flickered shadows against the opposite wall. Floor-to-ceiling bookcases, filled with leather-bound volumes of the great classics of literature, history, and philosophy lined two of the walls. On the third wall hung a large, square tapestry of a medieval battle, while against the fourth wall sat Franco's ornately carved oaken desk. Outside the casement window, a light snow fell steadily, its flakes forming lovely crystal patterns on the frosted panes.

Nico studied his surroundings with a blend of awe, respect, and surprise. This man whom he'd known only as teacher and farmhand was a man of great erudition. Yet, for as long as Nico had known him, he'd always comported himself humbly and without pretension. Even now, as he welcomed Nico to his modest quarters, his demeanor was that of a servant rather than a scholar.

Franco took a seat in a large, upholstered chair opposite Nico.

Nico's heart pounded. At last he would learn about who he really was from the one person who would best know.

But how to begin?

Nico looked at the middle-aged man sitting before him. The man who'd literally given him life and who now evoked a strange blend of disgust and admiration in Nico's soul. Nico's resemblance to him was striking. The same hairline. The same nose.

The same square chin.

Only their eyes were different.

A cold chill ran through Nico. Looking at Franco was like looking at himself in the mirror every morning.

"Thank you for inviting me to your home."

Franco's gaze was riveted on him. "Thank you for accepting my invitation. I've prayed for this day for a long, long time." His voice was wistful. Doleful.

Earnest.

Nico's heart warmed. "I can't honestly say as much, since I was but a boy when I left Sicily. But in the last several months, I have had a growing desire to understand the reason I seem to bear a great deal of resemblance to you." Nico inhaled deeply. "The night of *Nonna's* funeral, Mama told me the truth about you and about my relationship to you."

Franco raised an eyebrow. "I was wondering if you knew."

"I'm sorry she did not tell me sooner. It would have spared me a lot of anguish to have known the truth at an earlier age." He sighed. "Much, much anguish." Nico set his gaze steadily on Franco. "As it was, I was not surprised, as I had been noticing a resemblance to you for a while now. And, truth be told, I felt betrayed." Nico slowly rubbed his hands together. "But she was afraid, I guess. Embarrassed as well, I'm sure. It certainly could not have been a pleasant thing for her to have to convey such shameful news to her own son." Nico folded his hands between his knees. "But when you came to *Nonna's* funeral—for which I thank you—and then you invited me to visit you, Mama decided she could no longer postpone the inevitable. She would have to tell me the truth herself before I learned it some other way."

Franco listened, his gaze fixed intently on Nico. "I'm glad you know the truth now."

Nico leaned forward. "But I don't know all of it." He studied the man before him. "Would you be willing to answer some questions for me? Questions that have been troubling me for some time now?"

"Of course. But first, tell me what you know."

Dare Nico reveal the only memory he had of those early years? The memory that had left an unanswered question in his heart and still gnawed at him after all these years? "Yes. One thing stands out in my mind. A word the people would shout or mumble under their breath whenever Mama and I walked through the village."

"What was the word?"

Nico swallowed hard. Just thinking the word—let alone saying it—twisted his stomach. "*Bastardo.*" Nico lowered his voice to almost a whisper. "The word was *bastardo.*"

Franco's face contorted in pain as tears welled up in his eyes. He remained silent for a long time.

Nico squirmed in his chair. Had he offended Franco? Should he apologize? Ask leave of his natural father?

At last, Franco spoke, his voice trembling. "I did that to you. I, and I alone." He rubbed his hand over his face. "I am guilty of causing you that horrendous suffering." He lowered his eyes. "I am so very sorry, Nico. What I did to you is inexcusable. I can only imagine the pain I've caused you. Can you ever forgive me?"

A lump formed in Nico's throat. "Of course, I forgive you." The awkward moment turned sublime. Forgiveness always had a way of doing that, it seemed.

"*Grazie*." Franco smiled. It was a smile that reflected the deep gratitude of his heart. "Now, whatever you'd like to know, please ask. I will do my best to answer all of your questions, my son."

Nico's heart stirred. Franco's epithet had touched a place buried deep within him, a tender place never touched before. But dare he ask the question burning in his soul? "What made you do it?"

A tear streamed down Franco's cheek. "I was steeped in sin back then." His voice caught. "Selfish. Wicked."

"Unregenerate."

Nico studied his father's face. It was the face of a truly repentant man. A man who had suffered much because of his sin but who had sincerely turned away from it and asked God for forgiveness.

Franco's voice resonated in the room where they were seated. "At the time the horrific incident occurred, I was self-serving, prideful, and interested only in fulfilling my own lusts." He cleared his throat. "Sin will do that to a man, you know. Make him like an animal. Or, even worse, a beast." His face twisted in anguish at the memory.

"But did you love Mama at all?"

A gray shadow crossed Franco's face. "I was physically

attracted to your mother. But, no. I did not love her as a godly man loves a woman. Had I loved her, I would never have hurt her." Franco sighed. "Love does no evil."

Nico thought of Sofia and of his desire to do her only good all the days of his life. A sudden longing for her shook his soul. "I understand."

An awkward lull in the conversation ensued, broken by Franco's question. "Will you forgive me for hurting your Mama?"

The disgust Nico had felt toward this man who was his father suddenly waned. "Yes, I forgive you of that as well."

Franco lowered his gaze. "Thank you. I am not deserving of your forgiveness. Nor of the Lord's. Yet, I am most grateful for Jesus."

Nico swallowed hard. "Tell me about my roots. My origins. From where does our family come? What was your childhood like? Who were my grandparents? Great-grandparents?" Question after question poured out of Nico's heart.

For the next several hours, father and son communed. Nico asking questions. Franco answering them. Before Nico realized it, the clock struck midnight.

Yet, he felt as though the day had only just begun.

Chapter Ten

The day after the discussion over Mama's will, Maria stood by the large oaken dresser in Mama's room, sorting through Mama's belongings with her youngest sister, Luciana. The day was cloudy and cool, with a slight breeze blowing through the open window, bringing with it the aroma of orange and lemon blossoms from the budding groves on the hillsides below. A light drizzle had fallen since early morning, and darkening clouds threatened to grow into a major storm by early afternoon.

Maria's mind drifted to Nico. What was going on in his heart during this time he was spending with Don Franco? Had the two forged the beginnings of a genuine father-son relationship? Or had the truth about Franco's identity that she'd divulged to Nico colored the boy's relationship with his birth father?

The muscles of her stomach tightened. She'd find out soon enough. Tomorrow night, Nico would return from Milano. Then, the next day, she and her son would board the *Perugia* once again for their return trip to America. They'd have plenty of time to talk during the long return voyage.

Luciana placed one of Mama's dresses in the giveaway box. "It grieves me to think you will be leaving in two days. It seems as though you just arrived." The expression on Luciana's face revealed the depth of her pain.

Maria swallowed hard. "It grieves me, too, dear sister. The days I've been here have flown by."

"As time always does." A wistful look crossed Luciana's face.

"As a child, I used to think we had forever."

Luciana smiled. "That's because children live in eternal time. I think that is what Jesus meant when He said we must become like little children. He wants us to live with an eternal perspective on life, not a temporal one."

Maria pondered Luciana's wise words. "I'd never looked at that Scripture passage in that way. Your insights shed new light on it for me."

Luciana folded another of Mama's dresses and placed it in the box. "What will you do when you return to America?"

"First thing, as I mentioned to you and Cristina last night, I will talk to Luca about returning to Sicily."

Luciana stopped folding and smiled. "I hope he agrees. We have missed you terribly. Mama, especially."

The words pierced Maria's soul, although she knew Luciana had not spoken them in condemnation but in love. "I can only imagine the suffering Mama must have endured because of my departure."

Luciana placed a hand on Maria's arm. "She never condemned you, Maria. Mama was not like that. She just missed you. That's all."

"And I missed her, too. Terribly. When I got the news of her imminent death, I prayed fervently that I would get back in time to see her before she died."

"And, praise the Lord, you did." She smiled through welling tears. "God answered your prayer."

"Yes. God is good."

"Always." Luciana returned to her folding and placed another garment in the box. "Since we've decided to sell *Bella Terra,* where will you and Luca live if you move back? In Pisano? Ribera? Another village close by?"

Luciana's question hit Maria hard. She had not yet reconciled her sisters' decision to sell the farm with her own to keep it. "Luciana, to be honest with you, I still can't accept the decision to sell *Bella Terra*. So, to answer your question, I haven't thought of living anywhere else. In my mind and heart, if we return there is no place else to live but *Bella Terra*."

Luciana placed a finger on her cheek. She grew pensive. "Is there any way you and Luca can buy out Cristina's and my shares of the farm? Then you could live here."

Although Maria jumped at the idea, there was no way she and Luca could afford to purchase her sisters' shares of the farm. During their time in America, they had barely been able to survive on Luca's meager income and the few dollars she earned taking in sewing and mending.

"None that I can see." Maria's heart sank as she uttered the words. "We have been able to save very little."

Luciana resumed her sorting. "Speak with Luca, nonetheless, upon your return, and please write to me to let me know what he says." She paused and looked at Maria. "One never knows what the Lord will do." She smiled. "Meanwhile, I will be praying that Luca agrees to come home."

Come home. Luciana's words sounded so normal. So inviting.

So right.

Yes, returning to *Bella Terra* would mean coming home.

But would Luca think so? Or would he think returning to Sicily would be disobeying God? But what if their assignment in America were over? They'd spent long and difficult years trying to fulfill God's will, hadn't they? And what had it gotten them? No further along than when they'd arrived. In fact, they'd regressed, with no seeming hope of ever moving forward again. Luca was stuck in a job with little, if any, opportunity for advancement. His dream of opening his own tailor shop seemed far-fetched and impossible. Maria's dream of owning a home seemed just as impossible. And as for their children, there was no money for an education beyond high school. What would become of them?

"Thank you, Luciana. I will need all the prayers I can get. And, yes. I will write to you to let you know what Luca says. He is a reasonable man. At the same time, he is a man passionate to obey the will of God."

"That is a good thing. All the more reason to trust that if God is, indeed, calling you to return to Sicily, Luca will hear and obey Him."

Maria raised an eyebrow at the wisdom of Luciana's words. "You are full of remarkable insights today, dear sister of mine."

Luciana paused in her folding. "Thank you. Any wisdom I may have comes from the Lord. But beyond wisdom, I am full of deep love for you." With tears rolling down her cheeks, Luciana embraced her sister.

Maria and Luciana resumed their sorting of Mama's belongings.

Luciana's face lit up. "Maria, look! Here is Mama's Bible." Luciana handed the worn, leather-bound volume to her older sister.

Her heart pounding, Maria took it gently into her hands, caressing its faded black cover, sliding her fingers along the tattered edges of its thin pages. Ever since she'd made a decision to follow Christ shortly before Maria's birth, Mama had diligently sought to know God through this precious book. His handbook for living. His prescription for freedom.

His love letter to humanity.

Maria drew the Holy Book to her face and pressed it against her cheek. It smelled of lavender water, the same that Mama used to splash generously over her face and neck, especially on hot days. A sob rose to Maria's throat as she drank in the familiar fragrance.

"Would you like to have it?" Luciana smiled at her through tear-filled eyes.

"Oh, no! I could not take this, my dear sister. You keep it. You deserve it far more than I."

Luciana shook her head. "I'm sure Mama would want you to have it."

"How can you know?"

Luciana took the Sacred Book from Maria's hands and opened it. She searched through its pages and then stopped. "Read this." She pointed to Jeremiah 29:11: "'For I know the plans I have for you,' says the Lord. 'They are plans for good and not for disaster, to give you a future and a hope.'"

Maria furrowed her brows in question.

Luciana's gentle gaze met hers. "This was Mama's favorite verse. On the days she missed you the most, which was *every* day," Luciana chuckled through her tears, "she would quote this verse aloud and say, 'This promise is for my Maria. Even though I don't understand the reason she left us, I will trust in God's promise over her. I will trust that His plans for her are for good and not for evil, in order to give her a future and a hope.'"

Maria stifled a sob. Mama had thought of her every day. Every single day. It was more than she could say for herself about thinking of Mama. Remorse pierced her.

"Please, Maria. Take Mama's Bible." Luciana pressed the Holy Book into Maria's hands. "It will be a comfort to you in the months and years ahead. It will remind you of Mama's love for you." She smiled. "And of the Lord's."

The months and years ahead. What did those months and years ahead look like? Would they be spent in America, or would they be spent here in Sicily?

Maria took the Bible from her sister's extended hands. "Thank you." Her voice was barely a whisper. "Thank you more than I can ever adequately express. I feel as though I am taking a part of Mama back with me."

Luciana smiled and embraced her. "You are, Maria. A very big part. Indeed, you will be taking back with you Mama's whole life."

Maria swallowed hard and nodded. Yes, Jesus the Word was, indeed, Mama's whole life. And now Mama saw Him face-to-face, joyfully beholding the glory for which she had lived and in which she had died.

* * * *

His visit with Don Franco at an end, Nico left soon thereafter for his return trip to Sicily. He would take the night train from Milano to Naples, where he would then board the ferry to Palermo. From there, he would take the train to Ribera and then stop to visit Sofia before returning to *Bella Terra* to rejoin Mama.

The night was cool and dreary as he bid farewell to his father at the Milano train station in the wee hours of the morning. Travelers rushed to and fro, heading to trains that would take them in all directions, to all parts of Italy and beyond. Stationmasters shouted instructions for boarding amid tearful farewells, while departing trains left behind a trail of acrid fumes.

Nico stood before Franco. "Thank you for a wonderful visit."

His father placed a hand on Nico's shoulder. "It was my pleasure, my son." Franco's voice caught as tears filled his eyes. "Lord willing, we will see each other again soon."

Nico nodded, his throat tightening. "Yes. My plans are to move back to Sicily."

"And so are mine. Your decision to move back gives me even more incentive to do so." Franco smiled through his tears. "Besides, I've had enough of this dreary northern Italian weather. It has wreaked havoc on my old bones. I miss the warm, sunny climate of our magnificent island."

The train blew its whistle, alerting all passengers to board.

Nico took a step toward Franco. "I must go now. Good-bye." Impulsively, Nico embraced Franco.

His father held him close to his heart. "I release you to the will of God, my son."

Nico drew back and looked into Franco's eyes. "Thank you, *Papa*." The epithet slipped effortlessly from his heart and from his tongue.

Tears streamed down Franco's face. "Thank you. I never thought I would have the privilege of hearing you call me *Papa*."

Nico gave his father a final, tight embrace. "Until we see each other again in Sicily." He hesitated. "Soon, I hope." Then, without a further word, Nico quickly turned and boarded the train.

He walked down the narrow aisle and took a window seat from which he offered a final wave to his papa as the train pulled out of the terminal. The tear-laced smile on Franco's face engraved itself in Nico's memory. He would carry it in his heart for the rest of his life.

In a few moments, the train left the city, slowly rumbling out of the station before increasing its speed to a gentle, steady roar. Through the window, Nico gazed at the night sky. A bright moon cast shadows on the wintry countryside, illuminating patches of snow here and there, patches not too eager to thaw in submission to the coming rule of spring. In the distance, the majestic peaks of the Alps formed a magnificent backdrop to the snow-covered, rolling hillsides. Beneath him, the grating roar of the train's wheels on the iron tracks sent unsettling vibrations throughout his body as the train rocked back and forth, back and forth, rocking him with it.

He leaned his head against the back of the seat, pondering the events of the last two days. His visit with his biological father had transformed Nico's life. Answered many questions.

Raised even more.

Being with Franco had solidified his identity, his sense of self, his sense of purpose.

But it had also left him feeling confused. Angry.

Betrayed.

He clenched his fists on his lap. Why had Mama neglected to tell him the truth about his lineage? Did she think he'd never discover it on his own? Would she have told him had Nico not accompanied her to Sicily? How could he face Mama from now on with the same trust he'd had for her all of his growing-up years?

He squared his jaw.

The answer was plain and simple. He couldn't.

But he must!

A shiver coursed through his veins. At least Mama had been right about one thing. Don Franco was a new creation in Christ. How a man like him could have raped Mama lay beyond the scope of human comprehension. Franco was living proof that when one came to Christ, old things truly passed away. All things truly became new. Don Franco was, indeed, a new man. A godly man. He'd shown himself as such during Nico's visit with him. He was a man who loved his son and desired a close relationship with him. Franco had said so during their time together.

Nico, too, had felt the tug of their blood kinship. A kinship that, no matter what, could never be broken. His visit with his biological father had been eye-opening. Life-changing.

Heart-rending.

Nico closed his eyes. Over the past several days, his emotions had run the gamut from ecstasy in meeting Sofia, to painful revelation in spending time with Franco, to intense anger at Mama's betrayal. Now, as the train sped toward Naples, he rehearsed what he would say to her upon his return.

Nico drew in a deep breath as he struggled to piece together the fragments of his heart. He sighed. Franco was his real father. So, what about Nico's relationship with Luca? Would that change? If so, how?

Would Mama's confirmation that Franco was his biological father change anything between him and the man who had reared him as his own son? Would Nico's allegiance now be divided?

Would he be torn between two fathers?

And what about his mother? How could he feel the same toward her when she'd kept from him the very truth he'd needed the most? The truth about who he was.

The outskirts of the city soon gave way to the open countryside. Patches of snow dotted the barren ground. All of Italy suffered. Even the land. And when the land suffered, the people suffered.

Perhaps God would use him to restore the land.

The conductor approached him. "Ticket, please."

Nico reached deep into the pocket of his trousers, pulled out his crumpled ticket, and handed it to the conductor.

The conductor nodded. "Thank you." He looked at the destination on the ticket. "Are you Sicilian?"

Nico smiled. "Actually, I was born in Sicily but have lived in America for the past eight years."

"What brings you back to Italy? Surely, things are far better in America than they are here."

"My grandmother's illness. She died a few days ago."

The conductor's face grew solemn. "I'm sorry." He shook his head. 'Death is never an easy thing." He started to leave and then turned to address Nico again. "Is it worth going to America? I've been thinking of doing so myself. Things are quite bad here in Italy, as you have probably already seen."

"Your decision depends on one thing."

The conductor raised an eyebrow. "What's that?"

Nico fixed his gaze on the man. "It depends entirely on whether or not God wants you to go."

The man gave Nico a long, pensive look. "A thought-provoking answer."

"And the only one that will lead you in the right direction."

The man nodded and then left.

Truth be told, only two things were necessary in life: Hearing God's voice and obeying it. If one did those two things, one would never go wrong.

As Nico's eyelids grew heavy, sleep overtook him. Several hours later, he awakened to a rising sun in the east.

His thoughts returned to his visit with Franco. Ironically, in learning more about his earthly father, he'd acquired a new understanding of his heavenly Father. Although the world considered Nico a bastard, His heavenly Father considered him an adopted son. His heavenly Father approved of him, and that was the only approval he truly needed.

And now, his earthly father approved of him, too.

A warm sensation coursed through his veins. Despite his difficult beginnings, his future seemed promising.

He leaned his head against the back of the train seat. Sofia was ever present in his mind. When he'd told Franco of his love for her and of his intention to marry her, his father had been delighted. Now all that remained was to garner Mama's approval.

A feat easier said than done.

Chapter Eleven

While waiting for Nico to return from Milano, Maria spent the last day before her departure visiting the tiny village of Pisano in the valley below. It was there that, as a child, she'd gone to church every Sunday and on holy days. It was there she'd attended the Catholic school whose headmaster had been Don Franco.

It was there she'd met Luca.

It was also there she'd been raped and then shunned by the villagers.

What would she find on her visit today? Would anyone remember her?

Would she remember anyone?

The day was brisk and bright as Salvatore drove Maria in the old family wagon, its wheels creaking loudly as it made its way down the gravel road that led from *Bella Terra* to Pisano. A cool breeze swept across her face, leaving behind the fragrant aroma that always accompanied the citrus harvest—a season she remembered with fondness. In the nearby fields, small groups of farm laborers, wearing large-brimmed hats, sang old Sicilian folk tunes in harmony as they pick the ripened fruit. Overhead, a seagull dipped and soared, searching for food along the shores of the Mediterranean Sea.

Salvatore gently tapped Agostino, the old heavy draft horse, with his whip. "We had to get rid of Bianca shortly after you and Luca left for America."

Maria smiled wistfully. "Ah, yes, Bianca. How well I remember that gentle old mare. I learned to ride on her back when I could barely walk. How patient she was with me!"

Salvatore shook his head. "Losing her was one of the hardest things of my life." He sighed. "It's amazing how much one can grow to love an animal."

"You make me think of Nico and his love for Pippo." She glanced at Salvatore. "Nico was thrilled to discover his old puppy still at *Bella Terra*."

"I can only imagine."

"The best part was that Pippo remembered him."

Salvatore chuckled. "Once dogs learn a scent, they never forget it. They have long memories."

"Like people, no?" Maria chuckled.

"Only like people who won't forgive."

"Like some Sicilians, then." Sicilians had a reputation for holding grudges. Long grudges.

Ugly grudges.

Maria cringed. Would she find those long memories in Pisano?

Salvatore carefully guided the wagon into the village square. All around its perimeter, vendors stood by their carts, peddling their goods. Some carts boasted fresh fish from the sea. Clams. Mussels. Squid. Others were laden with oranges, lemons, and fennel. Still others, with broccoli, spinach, and winter squash.

In some ways, nothing had changed.

In other ways, everything had.

Salvatore brought the wagon to a halt. "I will let you off here and park the wagon at the far end of the square. When you've finished, you will find me there, probably taking a nap." He laughed.

Maria smiled. "Thank you, Salvatore. I won't be long. I plan to see who is left of those I knew. I should not be more than two hours."

"That's fine. Take your time. You know where I am."

Salvatore helped Maria descend and then drove the wagon to the edge of the square.

Clutching her purse, Maria took a deep breath and proceeded to walk across the square. Thirteen years before, she'd walked across this same square with little Nico in tow, on their way to his first day of school.

The horrid scene rose before her mind's eye. Ugly whispers filled the air. Whispers of "bastard," "harlot," and "whore." Her whole body trembled. She squeezed her son's hand more tightly. The hateful words started as whispers and then grew into a unified roar that still rang in her ears. She covered them, suddenly remembering that this was now and not then.

She exhaled a long sigh of relief and removed her palms from her ears.

"Excuse me, *Signora*." A fish vendor stopped her. "Are you all right?"

Startled and disoriented, she looked at him. "Yes. Yes. Why do you ask?"

"You seem a little lost, that's all."

"Thank you for your concern."

"No problem." He pointed to his fresh catch of the day. "By any chance, are you in need of some fresh fish? Just caught and delivered from the coast."

She glanced at the fish laid out in neat rows on the cart. "It looks good, but I'm not going straight home." Maria studied the man's face. "Angelo? Angelo Moroni?"

He gave her a questioning look. "Do we know each other?"

She smiled. "I am Maria. Maria Landro, wife of Luca Tonetta, the tailor."

Recognition lit up his gaze. "No! So, my eyes are not playing tricks on me. You looked familiar, but I could not place you." He shook her hand warmly. "How is my old friend Luca? Things have not been the same here in the square since he left for America." Angelo pointed toward Luca's old shop. "A florist now rents his old place."

Maria's gaze followed the direction of his pointing finger.

"He is well, thank you."

"Is he still tailoring?"

"No, unfortunately. He is working on the railroads."

"Tell him to move back to Sicily. We haven't had a good tailor since he left us."

Maria's heart warmed. Was Angelo's comment a sign from God? "Thank you, Angelo. I will tell him."

"What brings you back to Sicily?"

"My mother died a few days ago."

"Oh, I am so sorry."

"Thank you, Angelo." She drew in a deep breath. "And how is your family?"

He laughed. "My boys are taller than I, and my wife dotes on them as if they were still two-year-olds."

Maria joined in his laughter. "It's the syndrome of the Italian Mama."

"That it is. Your boy must be a man now."

So, Angelo remembered Nico. "Yes. He is nineteen years old. And Luca and I have two daughters as well—Valeria and Anna."

"Congratulations! You've done well for yourself considering—" He stopped in mid-sentence, suddenly recognizing his gaffe. An embarrassed look crossed his face.

Maria stiffened at Angelo's long memory. "Whatever good there is in my life has been the Lord's doing."

Angelo lowered his eyes. "I'm sorry, Maria. The past is the past, and we should let it rest." He looked at her with repentant eyes. "I'm glad to see that life has taken a better turn for you."

"Yes, the past is the past, and all is forgiven." She extended a hand toward him and smiled. "Well, I must be going. I'm so glad I got to see you, Angelo. May God bless you and your family."

"God bless you, too, Maria."

"Oh, regarding the fish—please put aside two pounds of

clams for me. I will pick them up on my way back. I need to make two more stops first."

"My pleasure, Maria." She turned to go.

"Maria?" Angelo called after her.

She looked back. "Yes?"

"I always knew you were innocent."

Tears sprang to her eyes. "Thank you, Angelo. That means more to me than you will ever know."

Nodding and smiling, the old fish vendor wiped a tear from his own eye and waved goodbye.

So, long memories did not always hold grudges.

Deeply moved, Maria directed her steps toward Luca's old shop. Her heart fluttered at the memory of the first time she'd entered the shop, looking for work, and met Luca.

Since they'd left, the front of the shop had been painted a dark shade of brown. Above the front window hung a tattered awning that seemed to have weathered many a storm. On the window hung a new sign: "Tonino's Flower Shoppe."

What would Luca think? After he'd been evicted for not paying his rent, Luca's dream of passing on his business to Nico had been destroyed. Could he revive it again? Would he want to?

She turned the knob and entered the shop. The fragrance of gardenias and roses filled the air and delighted her senses.

A young girl, about fifteen years of age, approached her. "Good afternoon, *Signora*. How may I help you?"

"Hello. You have a lovely shop here. Have you been here long?"

The girl gave her a suspicious look. "About eight years."

So this was the business that took over after Luca left.

"Why do you ask?"

Maria smiled. "You won't believe this, but my husband used to rent this space for his tailoring business."

The girl's eyes grew wide. "Really? But I don't recognize you. Are you from nearby?"

"Originally, yes. But now my husband, children, and I live in America."

The girl looked at her as though she'd met the Queen of Italy. "America! How I would love to go there!"

"Perhaps you will one day."

"What brings you back to Pisano?"

"My mother's illness. She died after we arrived."

"Oh, I am so sorry." The girl's compassion was genuine.

It was time for Maria to leave, but not before purchasing a flower. "I would like to buy one of your gardenias. It is my favorite flower."

The girl chose an especially lovely bloom, wrapped it gently in soft paper, and handed it to Maria.

"How much do I owe you?"

"Nothing." The girl smiled warmly. "Please accept it as a small gift in memory of former times."

Maria's heart swelled as tears rose to her eyes. "Thank you. You have no idea how much your kind gesture means to me." Impulsively, Maria gave her a quick embrace. "God bless you!"

"God bless you, too!"

On her way out, Maria turned. "What is your name?"

"Grace." The girl smiled. "My name is Grace."

Maria's heart stirred at yet another sign of God's love for her.

"Grace. A most beautiful name." With that, Maria left, her heart transformed by this unexpected encounter with God's grace.

She still had one very important stop to make before returning to Salvatore and the wagon. Despite her trepidation to go to the rectory, she could not leave without visiting Rosa.

Was the dear woman still alive?

* * * *

Leaving the square, Maria entered the narrow street that

led to the Church of the Virgin. Clutching her purse to her chest, she made her way down the pebbled street past the old schoolhouse. It seemed like only yesterday she'd brought Nico here for his first day of school. So much had happened since then.

She continued along the street and reached the church. The old medieval building was as beautiful as ever, with its ornate Baroque-style fountain in front of it. Parts of the fountain had chipped over the years, but that had not deterred the many pigeons still drinking from its waters.

A priest walked by, heading in the direction of the rectory that stood just beyond the church. From his robust frame and his slow gait, Maria recognized him as Don Vincenzo, the former assistant to Don Franco and now the pastor.

She quickened her pace to catch up to him. "Don Vincenzo!"

At the sound of her voice, the priest turned. "Yes? How may I help you?"

Maria quickly bridged the gap between them, and then, catching her breath, she stopped in front of him. "Don Vincenzo, do you remember me?" She smiled.

A look of recognition crossed his white-bearded face. "Why, if it isn't Maria Tonetta!" He took her hand and shook it heartily. "I was hoping I would get to see you before your return to America. I was told your mother died. My deepest condolences. Unfortunately, I could not attend the services. I had to be out of town to perform the wedding ceremony of my sister's son in Rome."

Maria returned his handshake. "Yes, Cristina told me. It's good to see you, Don Vincenzo."

"Likewise." He placed a hand on her shoulder. "Come. Come to the rectory. I'm sure Rosa would be thrilled to know you are here."

A sigh of relief escaped Maria's lips. "So, Rosa is still alive. Thank the Lord!"

"Yes, dear Rosa is now eighty-two years old and still serving faithfully."

Maria fell in stride with Don Vincenzo.

He turned his gaze toward her. "So, how is life in America treating you?"

Dare she tell him of the challenges she and Luca had faced? Of the poverty and prejudice?

Of her desire to return to Sicily?

"The Lord has been taking care of us." She would leave it to Don Vincenzo to read between the lines.

"The Lord has a way of doing that, doesn't He?"

As they approached the rectory, the aroma of sautéed garlic and freshly cooked *salsa* wafted through the air. Memories of Rosa's fine peasant cooking flooded Maria's soul. "I see Rosa is still making her famous spaghetti sauce."

"Indeed, she is." Don Vincenzo patted his ample stomach. "Can't you tell?" He laughed, and Maria was transported back to a time when her future seemed bright.

Until the rape.

The rectory held mixed emotions for her. Happy ones, with Rosa who'd been like a second mother to her. Horrific ones, with Don Franco, who'd turned her heaven into hell.

Don Vincenzo opened the back door and motioned her to precede him.

Maria found herself standing once again in the large rectory kitchen. Rosa stood at the old, black iron stove, her back toward Maria.

"Rosa, I have a surprise for you," Don Vincenzo called out.

The old woman turned slowly. In the many years since Maria had seen her, she'd aged considerably. Her body had grown frail, and her hair had turned white as snow. "What is it, Don Vincenzo?" Rosa's voice was the same, although its timbre had grown tremulous.

Maria broke into a smile as tears filled her eyes. "Rosa."

The old woman stood still in front of the iron stove, her mind trying to grasp the reality of what lay before her eyes. She squinted, trying to bring into focus the young woman who stood before her, and then her lips began to quiver. "Maria! My precious Maria!" Instantly, she opened her arms to receive the young woman who'd been like a daughter to her.

Maria ran into Rosa's arms and hugged her neck. "Rosa! Dear, sweet Rosa! How I have missed you!"

For several long moments, Maria nestled her head on Rosa's shoulder, listening to the old woman's feeble heartbeat. Then, lifting her head, Maria gazed into Rosa's kind eyes. The same kind eyes that had embraced her and comforted her during Maria's worst hour.

Rosa stepped back and held her at arms' length. "I never thought I would live to see the day when you would be standing in front of me again. God has given me a great gift."

"And me as well." Maria squeezed the old woman's gnarled hands. "Come. Let's sit for a few moments."

"I must make some coffee for you first."

"No, no, dear Rosa. Don't bother, please. I cannot stay long. Salvatore, my driver, is waiting for me in the village square. I want to make the most of our short time together."

Maria led Rosa to the kitchen table while Don Vincenzo left them alone and went to work in his office. The two women caught up on the past several years as Maria answered question after question about herself, Nico, Luca, and their two daughters. Finally, it was time to go.

Rosa stood. "Maria, there is something I want you to know before you leave."

"What is it, Rosa?" Maria studied the old woman's wrinkled face.

"Shortly after the—" she hesitated—"the incident, I was devastated for you. But I want you to know I never doubted your innocence." Her eyes filled with tears. "Not for one second."

Maria's heart overflowed with gratitude. Rosa was the second person that day to bless her with that revelation. "Thank you, Rosa. Thank you more than I can ever say."

"And now I must bid you farewell yet again." Rosa's voice quavered. 'But this time, dear one, it may be for the last time this side of Heaven."

Maria smiled. "Maybe not."

Rosa looked at her quizzically.

"I have been thinking of returning to Sicily. Since burying Mama, I have had a growing desire to come back to work the land. Otherwise, my sisters may have to sell *Bella Terra*."

Rosa sighed. "Oh, I do hope you can save *Bella Terra*. Does Luca want to return to Sicily?"

"He is reluctant to return, but I am planning to talk with him when I get back to Brooklyn. Perhaps he will change his mind."

Rosa nodded. "May God's will prevail."

"I will write to you and let you know." Maria kissed Rosa on both cheeks. "Please take care of yourself."

"And you do the same, my precious child."

With a squeeze of Rosa's hand, Maria took her leave, her heart heavy as she left her dear mentor and friend, perhaps for the last time.

A short while later, Maria bid a last farewell to Angelo as she picked up her order of clams. Then, she rejoined Salvatore and the waiting family wagon.

She hardly spoke on the trip back, so full was her heart from the day's healing encounters.

Chapter Twelve

Hours later, Nico found himself standing in front of Sofia's house. His knees shaking, he knocked tentatively at the front door. It was already early evening. The sun neared its descent toward the western horizon, casting long shadows across the surrounding hills of Ribera. In the distance, a blackbird sang the familiar song heard by locals during the waning days of winter called *Blackbird Days*.

Nico had decided that, on the way back from Milano to *Bella Terra*, he would visit Sofia. He had to see her one more time before his departure for America the next day—a departure the thought of which now caused his stomach to sicken. If there were any way to avoid returning to Brooklyn, he would do so in a heartbeat. But he must see his mother safely home. Love and duty demanded it. Once back in America, he'd arrange to return to Sicily as soon as possible.

His stomach tied in knots, Nico waited for someone to open the front door. His gaze scanned the property. The house was larger than most in the area. It was constructed of beautifully veined beige and green *Perlato di Sicilia* marble and located on an expansive, rectangular plot of land just outside Ribera. Around its perimeter stood shrubs of fragrant, winter daphne, their pale pink, tubular flowers surrounded by glossy, yellow-trimmed green leaves. It was obvious someone took great pride in maintaining the gardens.

Just as Nico considered knocking a second time, the sound of approaching footsteps from within the house made his heart lurch. His breath caught as he waited and rubbed clammy palms against his coat.

The heavy oaken door swung open, revealing a short, stocky, bald-headed man who looked to be in his mid-forties. His face was kind yet suspicious. "Yes?" The man knit his eyebrows into a question.

Nico's mouth grew dry. "Hello. You don't know me, but I know Sofia."

The man's eyes narrowed. "Oh, you do, do you?"

Nico swallowed hard. Not a very good start to a relationship. Apparently, this man was Sofia's father.

"And who are you?" The man's voice was gruff.

Nico took in a deep breath. "I am Nico Tonetta, the son of Maria Tonetta. My mother and father are old friends of Teresa Monastero, Sofia's mother."

The man's demeanor softened. "I see. So, your parents know my wife, Teresa."

"Yes. My mother and I are visiting from America. My grandmother, my mother's mother, died recently, and Teresa and Sofia came to the funeral to pay their respects."

The man nodded. "Yes, I remember now." His demeanor warmed as he extended a hand in welcome. "I am Sergio. Sergio Cosenza. Teresa's husband and Sofia's father." He opened the door all the way. "Come in. Come in, please."

"Thank you." Nico's heartbeat thundered in his ears. He needed to make a good impression on the father of the girl he loved.

And, one day, hoped to marry.

Nico entered the spacious foyer. An ornate fountain stood in one corner and a mid-sized flowering aloe plant in another.

Sergio closed the door. "Please. Follow me."

Nico followed Sofia's father down a hallway that led into a large airy living room overlooking a glass-enclosed garden. The room's tall windows allowed the late-afternoon sunshine to pour in, giving the entire space a cheery atmosphere. On the wall were paintings of the Sicilian countryside, with its rolling hills and lush vineyards.

Sergio motioned toward a tapestried sofa. "Please. Have a seat. I will go get Teresa and Sofia."

"Thank you." Nico took a seat on the sofa that faced the magnificent view of the garden. Brilliant with color despite the winter season, the garden boasted a large variety of plants and flowers, ranging from hyacinths to geraniums to violets, making it a veritable paradise. In the center of the garden, a statuesque fountain, featuring the figures of a man and a woman sitting under an umbrella, sounded like a splashing waterfall as its waters shot upward over the umbrella and then streamed down again into the pool below.

Nico's pulse raced. What would he say to Sofia? Would he be permitted to speak with her alone? Would his visit be construed as an affront or an impropriety? Having lived in America for so many years, he had no idea about the proper Sicilian etiquette for courting a young lady. What would Mama think if she saw him now? Perhaps he should have consulted her first. But there had been no time. They would be setting sail for America tomorrow. He had to see Sofia now or possibly lose his chance of marrying her.

The soft, swishing sound of long skirts caught Nico's attention, setting in motion the butterflies in his stomach. He rose, his knees wobbling. He fixed his gaze on the entrance to the living room. Teresa entered first, followed by Sofia. Sergio was the last to enter.

Nico's heart pounded wildly, threatening to burst through his chest.

"Nico! How lovely to see you again!" Teresa strode toward him, her arms open wide to receive him in a warm embrace.

"It's nice to see you again, too." Nico's gaze flew to Sofia's. "Hello, *Signorina* Cosenza." His insides quivered as his cracking voice betrayed his innermost feelings.

Sofia smiled. "Hello." Her eyes, glowing with pleasure, warmed his heart. "Please call me 'Sofia'."

Nico nodded. "And please call me 'Nico'."

Teresa quickly redeemed the awkward moment. "Please sit down so we can chat." She motioned Nico to the same sofa on which he had been waiting for the girl of his dreams.

Teresa sat beside him, with Sofia to her left. Sergio took a seat in a large Queen Anne chair adjacent to the sofa.

"So, what gives us the pleasure of your visit today?" Teresa's smile was warm and genuine.

Nico's tongue tied. He couldn't say he'd come because of his love for Sofia. Not yet, at least. So, what should he say? He hadn't planned for the eventuality of Teresa's question. "I am on my way home from Milano and, since Mama and I will be returning to America tomorrow, I wanted to stop by to bid you farewell." He studied Sofia's face, searching for any sign of sadness at his imminent departure. Her quivering lower lip told him all he needed to know. "I realize our visit the other day was interrupted by Mama's request that I help my *Zio* Pietro carry in more firewood, and I felt my sudden departure might have seemed rude." It was the best he could do to explain his visit now. But did Teresa see right through him? Did she read between the lines of his words?

Did she perceive the true reason for his visit? That he was in love with her daughter? That he needed to be with her one last time before returning to America?

Most important of all, did Sofia herself perceive his true motive in coming?

Nico gazed at her. Her dark, almond-shaped eyes mesmerized him with their beauty.

Teresa cleared her throat and smiled. "Well, whatever the reason, we are delighted to see you." She turned to Sofia. "Aren't we, Sofia?"

"Oh, yes. Yes, of course. I am most delighted to see you, Nico." The girl's face turned crimson.

Nico's heart soared at her use of the personal pronoun "I."

116

Teresa placed a hand on Nico's arm. "May I offer you some espresso?"

"Yes. Yes, thank you." Grateful that Teresa took charge of the conversation, Nico tensed when she left to make coffee. He gazed at Sofia's beautiful face. He wanted to memorize every feature, every nuance, every angle and carry the memory back with him to America. He drank in the rich color of her dark-brown eyes, the gentle upward tip of her nose, the elegant sweep of her high cheekbones, the soft curves of her soft, red lips. A sudden urge to kiss them threatened to overpower him.

Sergio cleared his throat. "So, tell me, Nico. What do you do in America?"

Shaken by the unexpected intensity of his desire, Nico drew his attention back to the moment and to Sergio. "I am a tailor by trade. I work in what is called the garment industry, a big clothing industry located in Manhattan. You've heard of Manhattan?"

"Yes. It is one of the five boroughs of New York City."

"Yes. You are correct. I am impressed that you know this since most Sicilians are unaware of that fact." No sooner had he spoken the words than Nico regretted them. Had he insulted the intelligence of the man who, he hoped, would one day be his father-in-law? Had he offended him by assuming that Sicilians were ignorant?

To Nico's great relief, a quick look at Sergio's face told Nico that all was well, that Sergio had not misinterpreted Nico's words but had, rather, taken them as the compliment Nico had intended them to be.

Sergio leaned back in his chair, crossed one knee over the other, and then took hold of his ankle. "Where did you learn the tailoring trade?"

"Actually, I learned it as a boy working with my father in his tailor shop in Pisano. And he learned the trade from his father before him. My father was one of the finest tailors in all of Sicily. People would come from far and wide to have him alter their clothes or make them a new suit of clothes." Was he saying too much too fast?

Sergio nodded. "Yes, I recall your father's name. His good reputation extended even to the other side of the mountain, where I grew up." Sergio formed a question with his brows. "If you don't mind my asking, why did your father leave Sicily, given that he was so well-established here on the island?"

Nico drew in a deep breath. "To be perfectly honest, *Signor* Cosenza, he left for two reasons. First, the economy in Sicily was collapsing. Because so many men were leaving for better opportunities, my father's business dwindled. A friend of his who had gone to America wrote to him saying there were numerous opportunities for tailors there. Second—and this is, perhaps, the most important reason—he left because he believed God was calling him to go to America to preach the Gospel."

A surprised look crossed Sergio's face. "Do you mean he left a lucrative business to become a missionary?"

"I guess you could say that. It was the main reason. But, as I said, the economy in Sicily was near collapse, forcing Papa to close his shop. So that fact contributed to his decision as well."

Sergio looked thoughtful. "I see." He rubbed his chin. "While I am not a deeply religious man myself, I admire men who are."

Nico's gaze kept wandering to Sofia's angelic face. Would he have the opportunity to speak with her before he left? To speak with her alone?

To tell her of his feelings for her?

He did not want to risk her not knowing he was in love with her and then marrying someone else. The very thought sickened him and filled him with dread.

Teresa soon returned with a tray on which were four ceramic demitasse cups, a pot of espresso, and a plate of Sicilian pastries. "At last." Her smile extended from ear to ear. "Some light refreshment for our honored guest." She emphasized the word "honored."

Teresa poured coffee for the four of them and then turned to Sofia. "Sofia, please offer Nico some pastries."

The blush on Sofia's face was like the blossoming of a delicate red tulip.

Nico's heart nearly burst out of his chest as Sofia rose, removed the plate of pastries from the tray, and walked toward him. The fragrance of orange blossoms emanating from her shapely body filled the air around him. A sudden thrill coursed through him as Sofia approached him.

Her hands trembled as she held the plate of pastries before him.

Nico reached for a small *cannolo*. "*Grazie.*" As he spoke the word, he gazed deep into Sofia's eyes, hoping she could read his heart.

The look she gave him told him she had.

The four of them engaged in lively conversation for about two hours. It was dark when Nico rose. "I must be going. Thank you so very much for your warm hospitality. Being with you this evening has been a highlight of my time in Sicily."

Sergio extended his hand. "It has been a pleasure to meet you, Nico. I do hope we get to see you again before too much time elapses."

"Yes! Before too much time elapses." Teresa repeated her husband's words.

Nico turned to Sofia. "It has been a joy to see you again, Sofia."

Teresa came to her daughter's side. "Sofia, why don't you see Nico to the door?"

Had Heaven given him all of Sicily for his own, Nico could not have been more ecstatic. He bid farewell to Teresa and Sergio and then followed Sofia to the front door.

119

She removed her coat from the coat rack, opened the door for Nico, and then followed him into the front garden, closing the door behind her.

They were alone—what Nico had desired the entire evening—although Sofia's father stood guard in the foyer just behind the door, his robust figure barely visible through the windowpane to the right of the door.

Nico stood before Sofia, his heart shifting like a violent earthquake. "Sofia, I will be leaving tomorrow, but before I leave, I must tell you two things. First, I must tell you that I have feelings for you. Strong feelings." He studied her face for the impact of his words on her. "Sofia, I am in love with you."

Sofia's eyes welled up with tears. "Nico, I have strong feelings for you, too. Ever since I first saw you at *Bella Terra*."

He stuffed his hands into his pockets. "The second thing I must tell you is that I have decided to move back to Sicily."

Her eyes widened with joy.

"If I could remain now, I would. But I must first return to America. I cannot let Mama make the return trip alone. Besides, there are a few things I need to take care of before leaving Brooklyn. I will have to quit my job, say goodbye to a few friends, and—"

"And what, Nico?"

"And tell Mama and Luca that I've decided to return."

"You haven't told them yet?"

Nico shook his head. "That will be the most difficult part." Should he tell Sofia now about Don Franco? "Sofia, you know Luca is not my real father."

Sofia nodded. "My mother said as much at your grandmother's funeral."

"You knew, then?"

"Only what Mama mentioned at the funeral. She has not yet explained further."

So, all these years. Teresa must have known about Nico's

past as well. Would Teresa's knowing affect his future relationship with her daughter?

Nico continued. "I just returned from a visit with my biological father. I want to move back to Sicily to get to know him better." Nico gazed into her eyes. "To get to know myself better."

Sofia lowered her eyes. "How about getting to know me better?"

What a fool he was! "Of course, dear one! Of course, I want to get to know you better! How stupid of me! I want to return because of you—and because of these other things."

Sofia lowered her eyes. "So, you are not returning mostly because you love me?"

Nico's heart clenched. He'd said something wrong. "That, too!"

"That, too? It is not your main reason for returning to Sicily?"

Nico's brain reeled. "Should it be?"

Sofia's gaze met his. "I think it should be. If it isn't, how can I be sure you truly love me?"

Was this their first lovers' spat? He couldn't leave Sicily while at odds with Sofia.

He went to reach for her hand but withdrew, suddenly remembering her father who watched them through the window. "Sofia, I love you with all of my heart. Yes, I want to return to Sicily because I love you. But I refuse to lie to you by not telling you that I also want to return to discover who I am. To discover my true roots. For many years, I have lived as Luca Tonetta's son, but I have never been certain of the identity of my biological father. Now I am certain I am the son of Don Franco Malbone." Nico lowered his voice to a whisper. "The man who raped my mother."

Sofia clamped a hand on her mouth to stifle a gasp. "Oh, Nico! I am so sorry! I did not know."

"I'm sure your mother would have told you the whole story sooner or later."

Her gaze revealed deep compassion.

"Sofia, listen to me. I came to your home today because I'm in love with you. I will return because I'm in love with you. I will return because I also want a relationship with my biological father. I will return because I also want to come back to my roots. To discover who I really am." He swallowed hard. "I can't be more honest with you than that."

"I see."

"But do you understand?"

She gazed into his eyes. "Yes, Nico. *Capisco*. I truly understand."

A flood of warmth rushed through his veins.

The moon cast purple swaths of light across the front lawn. "I must go. May I write to you from America?"

She nodded. "When will I see you again?"

"Not soon enough. I will do my best to wrap things up in New York." He wanted to kiss her on the cheek but did not dare, with her father watching just inside the door. "I will write to you as soon as I get back to Brooklyn. My return address will be on the letter, so you will know where to respond to me."

He shook her hand warmly. "Until next time, my love." The words caught on the lump in his throat.

"Until next time." Tears streamed down Sofia's cheeks.

He walked away and then turned to wave at her. The image of her beautiful figure standing in front of the flowering daphne shrubs would sustain him until the day he would return to make her his wife.

But he had much to do between now and then.

Including turning Mama's world upside down with his life-changing decision to move back to Sicily.

* * * *

Maria sat alone in Mama's old rocking chair on the back veranda of *Bella Terra*, awaiting Nico's return. Night had fallen, revealing a dazzling blanket of stars across the velvet-blue Sicilian sky. Maria gazed at them in wonder. Not once had she seen such brilliant stars in Brooklyn. Most of the time, a cloud of industrial haze covered the sky. Worse than that, it seemed a cloud of human indifference to God's magnificent creation covered the American soul.

Would she ever fit in with her new homeland?

She inhaled the sweet fragrances of almonds and citrus, so prevalent this time of year on this part of the island. Fragrances she'd sorely missed. How often had she clipped a cluster of almond blossoms to place on the kitchen table! Mama loved almond blossoms and always brightened whenever Maria brought some inside. Perhaps she could bring back some seedlings to grace her somber flat in Brooklyn.

A dog barked in the distance. Her stomach tensing, she folded her hands and accelerated her rocking. Nico should have been back by now. Where was he?

She wrestled the horrific thoughts that bombarded her mind. Had he missed the train? Had he been in an accident?

Had he been overtaken by highway robbers? Despite his age, he'd never traveled alone in Italy before. Would he be alert to the nuances of a culture he'd left behind as a boy? A culture fraught with hidden dangers?

A culture he really did not understand?

Wringing her hands, she forced herself to silence her mind. To focus on other things.

To trust God.

A meadow pipit trilled in the distance.

Her mind shifted to Don Franco. Had her son's visit with his birth father gone well? Or had their meeting after so many years of separation been strained? Distant?

A failure?

Ashamed of herself, Maria secretly hoped nothing would come of Nico's reconnection to the former priest. That the boy's growing desire to know his birth father would melt into nothing more than a passing fancy. That his visit with Franco would satisfy a temporary need so Nico could move on with his life.

And she with hers.

But deep down, she feared that his reconnection to Franco would mean the emotional loss of her son to his birth father. A weakening of the deep bond she'd had with Nico all his life.

A reconnection of her own life with the man who'd raped her.

She cringed at the thought. It was one thing to have Franco work on the farm as a laborer. It was quite another to have him involved in the personal life of her family. Forgiveness did not necessarily mean intimacy.

A wild rabbit hopped across the gravel at the foot of the veranda, the animal's long ears flickering in the moonlight. It stopped short, looked at her, and then scurried into the darkness.

Since she'd been in Sicily, anxiety about her only son had mounted. Why? She wasn't sure. Perhaps it had to do with Franco's return into the boy's life. Truth be told, she didn't like it. Not one bit. Yes, Franco had a right to a relationship with his son, but that didn't mean Maria had to like the fact. After all, they'd managed perfectly well over the years without Franco's presence. Not that she'd resented their relationship when Nico was a boy on the farm. Back then, her son hadn't known of his true relationship with Franco. Nico had looked on him only as a teacher and friend.

So, why did she feel differently now? Why did Franco's re-entrance into their lives trouble her so much? Perhaps it was that Nico had desired the renewed relationship, learning at last that Franco was his biological father. Had her failure to tell her son the truth been due to her subconscious unwillingness to share him with his birth father?

To keep her son entirely to herself?

The selfish thought unnerved her, sending waves of guilt throughout her flesh.

She tensed. Perhaps it was that her own fear of letting go of the son who had become her life revealed the ugly truth that she was a controlling, overbearing, possessive mother more concerned about meeting her own need than the need of her son.

Shifting in her rocking chair, she drew a deep breath.

And then there was Sofia. Her appearance in Nico's life had only compounded and complicated Maria's concern about losing him. Clearly, he was smitten with the girl. Of all the young women in the world to fall in love with, why did it have to be Teresa's daughter?

Her stomach in knots, Maria leaned back in the rocking chair, trying to sort out the turmoil in her soul. Two people whom she'd wanted to keep at bay had re-entered her life. And both of them threatened to take her son from her.

A rustling sound against the nearby bushes caught her attention. "Mama, what are you doing up so late?"

Nico's welcome voice calmed her fears. "I'm waiting for you." Maria exhaled a sigh of relief.

He climbed up the three steps to the veranda and gave her a peck on the cheek. Then he sat down in a chair beside her and smiled. "Were you worried about me?"

The light of the moon on his boyish face warmed her heart. "Yes."

"But why, Mama? I'm a grown man."

She deflected his question. "Tell me about your visit with Don Franco."

Nico settled back in the rocking chair. "I enjoyed it very much."

Maria's heart sank. "How did you feel about reconnecting with him?"

"Oh, Mama. It seemed so natural. So right. So comforting. We talked for hours."

She stiffened. "Did you learn what you went there to learn?"

"Yes, and much, much more."

"'Much, much more'?" Nico's words pricked her soul.

"Yes. Not only did I learn about my ancestry as far back as Don Franco knew it, but I also learned that he is a learned man of great wisdom. As were many of my forefathers."

"And?"

Nico turned his gaze toward her, his eyebrows furrowing into a question. "And I am happy he is my father."

Maria's muscles tensed. "*Luca* is your father." Her words were slow and deliberate.

A frown crossed Nico's face. "Mama, please. I mean no disrespect toward Papa. He took me in when I was fatherless and raised me as his own son. For that I will be forever grateful to him." He paused. "But he is not my biological father. By saying so, I am not renouncing him, nor am I being ungrateful for what he has done for me."

Maria rose and paced back and forth on the veranda. A chilling breeze blew across her face, adding to the growing chill in her heart. "So, are you saying you are happy the man who raped your mother is your father?"

Nico leaned forward and placed his folded hands between his knees. "Mama, I'm very sorry about the rape, but Franco is no longer the same man. He has repented. And you yourself said you have forgiven him."

Nico was right. She had forgiven Franco. But was she still holding his sin against him? If so, she had not truly forgiven him. She drew in a deep breath. "Yes, I have forgiven him." She stopped pacing and returned to her rocking chair.

"Then why are you so troubled about what I choose to call him?"

She pondered Nico's question. "I guess it's that Franco has not been involved in your life for most of your life, and Luca has. It seems that Luca should rightfully bear the title of *papa*."

"I think Luca is mature enough to understand."

Maria flinched. Had her sensitive son suddenly become hardened? "Are you saying you will no longer call Luca your papa? That you will now call Franco your papa?"

"In a way, yes."

"There's no 'in a way' about it, Nico! Either Luca is your papa, or he is not."

"Mama, don't you think it's about time you treated me like a grown man, capable of making my own decisions?"

What had happened to her usually pliant and compliant son? This was new behavior from him. Disconcerting behavior.

Unnerving behavior.

Maria's blood grew hot. "This is not about treating you like a grown man. It's about respecting the man who raised you, in spite of the fact that he isn't your biological father."

"I do respect Luca. I simply don't want to call him *papa* any longer because I have discovered who my real papa is."

She'd reached a stalemate. Better to back off now—at least for the time being—than risk losing her son's heart. "Very well. If you no longer want to call Luca your papa, then you will have to tell him so yourself."

"I plan to, Mama. As soon as we get back to Brooklyn." Nico's gaze met hers. "I know he will understand."

"You may think you know. But you don't know your father."

Nico's voice rose slightly. "He is not my father."

Every muscle in her body stiffened. This conversation was going nowhere.

Nico leaned forward. "Mama, what is really troubling you?"

His question stung. "I'm not quite sure."

"Could it be that you cannot let go of me?"

Her son's insight pricked her conscience. Nico had always been a perceptive child, capable of striking at the heart of a problem.

Guilt washed over her. She stopped rocking. "Why do you think I can't let go of you?"

Nico folded his hands between his knees. "Don't you see that you are trying to impose your views on me? That you're trying to get me to do something I don't want to do?" His gaze met hers. "I'm no longer a child, Mama. While I will always do my best to respect you, I can no longer allow you to control me. I need you to understand that."

Maria turned and walked to the edge of the veranda. Why was it so difficult to let go of her hold on her son? What kind of mother was she?

She'd always thought she was a good mother. Wise. Discerning.

Just.

Yet, this situation with Nico, which now extended to Franco and Sofia, had exposed ugly traits she hated to admit to herself. Traits like envy and jealousy. Control and manipulation.

Selfishness and fear.

If she were totally honest, she didn't like what she saw coming to the surface from the hidden places of her heart.

But she felt powerless to change.

Chapter Thirteen

The euphoria of his recent visit with Sofia dissipated as Nico listened to Mama's complaints about his relationship with Don Franco. Yes, they were complaints, for Mama had no rational basis for them. What did it matter to her if he wanted a relationship with his biological father? She should be happy for him, not obsessed with fear.

And her worries about Luca were unfounded. Calling Franco *papa* would in no way diminish his love and respect for Luca. Nor would it diminish Luca's love for Nico.

Of course, Nico would speak with Luca about it upon their return to Brooklyn, but Luca would understand. He was, after all, a man, too.

The hour grew late as Nico sat in the rocking chair next to Mama. A full moon hung low in the indigo sky, partially covered by a white cloud that sailed across its brilliant surface. At the moon's side, Venus glowed brightly.

Nico's body, drained with the fatigue from a full day of travel, beckoned for sleep, while his soul beckoned for understanding from Mama. He drew in a deep breath, marveling at Mama's strange behavior. It was unlike her to be so unreasonable. So adamant.

So unbending.

Her irrational behavior created an unusual tension between them—a tension they'd never known in their relationship. Perhaps the reason was that, until now, he'd always been compliant. Always agreed with Mama's way of doing things.

Always obeyed her.

But he was a man now. And a man had to break away

from his mother's influence in order to thrive as a man. Besides, now that he planned to marry Sofia, he would have to leave Mama emotionally and cleave to his wife. The Holy Scriptures commanded as much.

He leaned back in the old rocking chair, silent as he collected his thoughts. Nearby, a barn swallow chirped the same evening song its ancestors had chirped for centuries. The sound was soothing to Nico's troubled soul.

Standing at the edge of the veranda, Mama turned toward him. "And then there's the matter of Sofia."

Nico's muscles stiffened. "What about Sofia?"

"What are your feelings toward her?"

"I love her, and I want to marry her."

Mama's countenance grew dark. "I forbid you to marry her."

Mama's demand ignited a fire in Nico's belly. He stood to his full stature. "I'm sorry, Mama, but you can't forbid me to marry Sofia. Or any woman, for that matter. Now that I am an adult, you no longer have that right. That decision is mine and mine alone."

Mama's face turned pale. Her jaw squaring, she pointed an index finger at him. "As long as you live under my roof, you will do what I say. Is that clear?"

Nico swallowed hard. This was not the same Mama he'd known all his life. Not the same Mama who'd raised him in kindness and gentleness. What was happening to her? "No, it's not clear at all, Mama. What's clear is that you are trying to control me, and I won't have it."

Mama drew closer to him. "Do you dare rebel against your own mother?"

Nico's heart sank. He balled his hands into tight fists, trying hard to control the negative emotions raging within him. "Mama, you must believe me when I say it is not my intention or my desire to rebel against you. But there comes a time in a man's life when he has to break away from his mother's apron strings. And for me, that time is now."

Mama placed her hands on her hips. Her gaze was stern. "Oh, so you feel as though I've tied you to my apron strings?"

He softened his voice. "You have, Mama. Can't you see that you have?"

She remained unflinching. "All I see is the many years I've sacrificed to give you a good life. And this is the thanks I get." Folding her arms across her chest, she turned away from him and returned to the edge of the veranda.

A crow cawed in the distance.

Nico raked trembling fingers through his hair. The situation seemed hopeless. Mama had made up her mind, and there was no changing it.

"Mama, I'm thankful for all you've done for me. You are a wonderful mother. But for some reason, I can't get through to you about my need to be free. To make my own decisions for my life.

He sighed. "To be a man."

Mama remained silent.

"Please try to understand, Mama."

Nico waited, but still she did not reply.

"Have you nothing more to say, Mama?"

"Nothing."

"Please, Mama. Please try to understand my viewpoint."

"There is nothing more to understand, Nico. I've spoken my mind, and I won't change it."

He shook his head in despair. "I'm going to bed."

And with that, he went into the house, leaving Mama alone with her thoughts.

* * * *

Several hours after accompanying Nico to the train station, Don Franco walked across the campus to his classroom. The time he'd spent with his son had filled a deep and longstanding void in his heart. But not only filled it. His visit had created a new hunger to be close to Nico for the rest of his life. Franco would love nothing more than to have him in Italy. To make up for lost time. Lost years.

Lost dreams.

Now that they'd reconnected as father and son, Franco's life would never be the same.

A white winter sky hung overhead as thick flakes fell to earth. Yet, despite the cold, February weather, spring had already arrived in Franco's heart.

He breathed a prayer of thanksgiving to the God Who, in His time, made all things new.

The God Who'd restored his son to him and him to his son.

He and Nico had spoken for hours about the past, the present, and the future. Nico's desire to return to Sicily had fanned Franco's hopes that his son would, indeed, decide to return to the land of his roots, thereby enabling Franco to share more intimately in Nico's life.

What an answer to prayer that would be!

For years, he'd prayed that God would restore Nico to his life. Not for Franco's benefit—although that certainly played into his request—but for Nico's benefit. Franco wanted to make up to his son for all the pain and suffering he'd caused him by siring him through rape and out of wedlock. The curse of illegitimacy was not only a social curse but a spiritual one as well, a curse that could be broken only by the power of Jesus Christ.

Franco shuddered as he tugged the collar of his woolen coat more tightly around his neck. A new winter storm was blowing in from the north, leaving in its wake several inches of fresh snow and a bitter wind that took one's breath away. Hastening toward the school building, he spotted a doe running across the campus. Frightened by Franco's sudden appearance, the beautiful young animal halted for a moment and then darted into the safety of the adjacent woods.

"*Professore! Professore!*"

At the sound of Matteo's voice, Franco turned. His student hurried across the lawn, pushing through the thickly falling flakes.

"Matteo, you are back! It is so good to see you again. How are you doing?"

The young man loped across the last few meters between him and Franco. "Doing as well as can be expected, sir. I'm glad to be back."

Franco placed a hand on the young man's shoulder. "How are things at home?"

"Settled down a bit now. We buried Papa, and I stayed with Mama for a couple of days. My older sister has taken Mama into her home, so I am now at peace that Mama will not be alone."

"Thank the Lord. I was concerned you might not be able to resume your studies."

"I was, too." Matteo smiled. "Well, I must get some breakfast, *Professore*. I will see you in class later this morning."

Franco nodded. "Yes. We'll resume our philosophical discussions."

Matteo's face grew serious. "Since Papa's death, I have been thinking a lot more about God, death, and the afterlife."

"This is a good thing. A very good thing."

Matteo nodded. "I would like to talk with you more about it."

"Yes. Yes, indeed."

Franco watched as Matteo made his way through the falling snow across the campus to the cafeteria. Interesting how the death of a loved one often set one on the path of truth—if, that is, one was sincerely seeking truth. Matteo was such a one.

God willing, Franco would help him discover the truth he sought.

Bracing himself against the growing wind, Franco continued toward his classroom. He entered the old building and wiped his boots on the mat just inside the door.

His thoughts went back to Nico. Once his son returned, Franco himself would move back to Sicily in order to be near him.

And to his future grandchildren.

His heart warmed at the prospect and at God's great mercy in granting him this desire of his heart.

But a nagging thought assailed his brain. What would Maria and Luca think of Nico's decision to return to Sicily?

And of Franco's intimate intrusion into Nico's life?

Chapter Fourteen

The day of Maria and Nico's departure arrived before she was ready for it. The final decision regarding the sale of *Bella Terra* had been postponed pending Maria's discussion with Luca upon her return to Brooklyn. As soon as Luca gave her an answer, she would write to her sisters. If Luca agreed to move back, then he and Maria would live on the farm and do their best to bring it back to solvency. If Luca refused to move back, then Maria's sisters would be free to proceed with the sale of the farm.

Bidding farewell to Pietro, Cristina, and Luciana at the Port of Palermo, Maria wiped streaming tears from her face. Would that she could just as easily wipe the sorrow and grief from her heart!

The day was gray and somber, fueling the grayness of her soul. Ominous clouds moved in from the west, portending a storm. Overhead, a single seagull flapped its wings as it dove toward the water and crested on a wave.

Maria held her youngest sister's hand in both of her own. "You must come visit us some time."

"I would like that very much." Luciana smiled.

"Unless, of course, we move back to Sicily first."

"That would be even better. I'm not too fond of traveling by ship. I get seasick very easily, although I would make the trip to see you." Luciana smiled through her tears. "Meanwhile, know that I will be praying for you, my dear sister." Luciana's eyes filled with tears.

"And I for you." Maria embraced Luciana tightly, wondering when—and if—she would see her sister again.

135

Then Maria turned to Cristina. "And you, dear Cristina, take care of yourself and your soon-to-be-born little one." Maria gently touched Cristina's growing belly. "Write to me as soon as the baby is born. I want to know if I am *zia* to a niece or a nephew. Whichever—boy or girl—your child will be a great blessing!"

"Yes. I will write without fail." Her voice quavered. "I love you so very much, Maria!"

"And I you, dear sister of mine!" Maria enfolded her sister in a tight embrace.

The sound of the foghorn startled Maria. "Nico, it's time." Giving Luciana, Cristina, and Pietro one last hug, Maria swallowed the sob that rushed to her throat. Part of her did not want to leave, yet part of her longed to be back with Luca, Valeria, and Anna.

Conflict. It was the endless and tormenting emotional state of the immigrant's soul. A soul torn between two lands and two families. Between one's roots and one's dream.

Between one's desire and one's destiny.

Why could they not be one and the same?

She'd witnessed this conflict over and over again in her Italian compatriots in Brooklyn. A conflict that kept them in continual limbo over their identity. While their minds lived in the present, their souls lived in the past. While their bodies lived in the New World, their hearts lived in the land of their birth. While their reason addressed the challenges of their new surroundings, their emotions remained tethered to the memories of yesterday.

Only the children born to them in their new homeland seemed able to escape this emotional tug-of-war. At least, some of it. For these same children heard their parents' stories again and again, absorbing them to a great extent into their own beings. Perhaps only the third generation would be able to break totally free.

But not only had Maria witnessed the conflict, she'd lived it herself day in and day out. Was she Italian? American? Somewhere in between? Could her past and her present be reconciled into a future that would bring her lasting peace?

She sighed and picked up the basket of food Luciana had prepared for them, and, taking Nico by the arm, she turned toward the gangplank.

Already dozens of passengers, laden with baskets and canvas bags filled with personal belongings, thronged onto the ship. The pungent smell of garlic permeated the air, mingling with the smell of squid, mussels, and tuna from the sea vessels unloading their day's catch farther down the pier. The shouts of rugged fishermen competed with the doleful sobbing of those leaving their families for good.

Maria's heart clenched.

Like herself eight years earlier, many were emigrating for the first time to America, their hearts filled with the hopes and dreams of a better life. Men and women, young and old. Some traveling alone. Some with spouses and children.

Some with friends and fellow villagers.

In all of their faces she read the hope she'd once shared. A hope that had been shattered over and over again when the reality of daily life in America, with all its challenges and setbacks, set in.

Maria's heart sank. Should she warn these precious people—her countrymen—about what really awaited them in the New World? About the hardships and disappointments?

The loneliness and alienation from mainstream society?

The poverty and prejudice? The hopelessness and hate?

No. That would be cruel and heartless. Besides, perhaps some of them would face a better fate than she and Luca had faced. Perhaps they would not miss their homeland as much as she missed hers.

Perhaps they might even forget the country they were leaving behind.

Reaching the deck, she whispered a prayer of blessing upon them and wished them well.

A bright sun beat down on the aging vessel, slightly mitigated by a brisk breeze that blew in from the Mediterranean Sea. Maria took a deep breath of the fresh salt air, hoping it would give her strength for the long trip ahead.

In a few moments, she and Nico found a place along the railing from which they could wave farewell one last time to Luciana, Cristina, and Pietro. Amid the hundreds of people bidding farewell to their loved ones, Maria found her sisters and brother-in-law in the crowd and waved goodbye. Spasms of grief twisted her heart. This time, Mama was not among them. This time, Mama would not have to experience and endure the deep anguish of losing her daughter to another land.

This time, Mama was at peace.

A sudden thought crossed Maria's mind. How would she herself feel if Nico did, indeed, marry Sofia and move back to Sicily, leaving her little hope of ever seeing him again?

She dismissed the troubling thought. That one of her children would return to Sicily was such a remote possibility that it was virtually non-existent. She had nothing to fear. The New World had become their homeland. Indeed, why would any of them want to leave it at this point?

She sighed as a yearning filled her soul. The only way her children would return to Sicily would be if she and Luca returned to Sicily.

But Luca would never agree to return.

Or would he?

She turned to Nico. "I'm so glad we came."

"I am, too, Mama. Now you will not live with any regrets about not having seen *Nonna* before she died."

Nico was right. But what about the other regrets she was living with? Regrets about leaving Sicily? About leaving *Bella Terra*? About missing eight years of living near Mama? Of not being by her side during her most difficult times? Would her children one day share those same regrets?

Probably not. Maria was the transition generation. The generation torn between two worlds. The generation that would suffer most before its progeny would be assimilated into the culture of its adopted land.

The generation ripped in two.

As the ship left port, Maria watched her family recede into the background. The foghorn blasted again as the *Perugia* pulled out of Palermo Harbor. Choking back sobs, Maria waved a final farewell to Luciana, Cristina, and Pietro before the ship made a westward turn.

Wiping hot tears from her eyes, she sighed and looked at Nico. "It will be good to get home."

But the distraught look on her son's face made her muscles tense. "Will it not?"

His failure to reply shook her to the depths of her soul.

* * * *

Two days later, the *Perugia* approached the Rock of Gibraltar. After Mama had retired for the night, Nico went up on deck to get some fresh air. Everywhere people slept, wrapped in blankets to protect themselves from the night chill. Conditions below in steerage were so deplorable one had to go up on deck to breathe clean air. Here and there, passengers paced the deck in a futile attempt to ward off seasickness.

A full moon shone in the night sky, casting its bright beams across the dark, rippling waters of the Mediterranean Sea. Soon they would near the Strait of Gibraltar that would lead them into the rough, wintry waters of the Atlantic Ocean.

Nico's thoughts drifted to Sofia. Was she watching the same full moon from her bedroom window? Was she thinking about him with the same passion with which he was thinking about her?

Did she miss him with the same longing with which he missed her?

A seagull glided down from the night sky and perched on the railing next to him. Nico imagined the sleek, white-breasted creature carrying a message from him to Sofia. He pictured Sofia receiving the messenger seagull into her smooth, beautiful hands with delight, removing the slip of paper from its beak, and then pressing it to her lips before reading it. He could see the smile on her sensuous lips as she read his words of love sent from afar.

Nico leaned his arms on the railing and spoke softly to the seagull. "Hello, my little friend. When you fly back to Sicily, would you find my Sofia and tell her I miss her?" Nico gulped. "And I love her." The words came out in a hoarse whisper.

His heart ached. Oh, the silly imaginings of love that would wish a seagull would carry a message to one's beloved! One day soon, Nico would return to Sicily himself and convey not only this message but an even weightier one to Sofia.

One day soon, he would ask her to marry him.

He filled his lungs with a deep breath of the fresh ocean air. Salt spray landed on his face like dew on morning glories. He watched the ship's foamy wake, churning amid the blue-gray waves that gently rocked the boat back and forth, back and forth. Perhaps, if he remained on deck long enough, he'd get to see the Rock of Gibraltar. Symbol of strength and steadfastness.

That's what he wanted to be for Sofia. A rock of strength.

I am the Rock. The Lord's words rose from the depths of his spirit. *I alone am Your Strength.*

"Yes, Lord," Nico whispered into the cold night air. Only by relying on the true Rock could he be a rock to his future wife.

His mind returned to Mama. After their strained conversation upon his return from Milano three nights before, they'd spoken to each other only in generalities about mundane

140

matters. Preparing for their return trip. The weather. The economy of Sicily. But underneath the surface still lay deep issues between them that had yet to be resolved.

Perhaps he'd better wait until they were back in Brooklyn to resolve them. Luca would help temper Mama's anger and inject balance into a situation that had lost balance.

Besides, Luca and Mama would need each other's support to handle the shocking news that Nico would be leaving Brooklyn to build a life with Sofia in Sicily.

But what if Luca also frowned upon his decision? What if Luca also tried to dissuade him?

What if Luca joined Mama in forbidding him to move back?

Nico's stomach clenched. He pushed aside the unpleasant thought. Chances were that Luca would understand. But Mama was the problem. That she did not understand stunned him. Had not Mama's own mother strongly objected when Mama and Luca decided to come to America? Yet, despite her own mother's objections, Mama had left. Why could she not allow him to do likewise?

A shout from one of the passengers diverted his attention. "The Rock! The Rock of Gibraltar!"

At the man's words, Nico turned his gaze toward the enormous, monolithic rock formation to the right side of the ship.

Nico's gaze rose toward the massive rock. Towering into the night sky, it stood in stark contrast to the smallness of the *Perugia*. When Nico was but a lad in primary school, Don Franco had taught him that Gibraltar was thought to be one of the Pillars of the mythical Hercules and the limit of the then-known world. Nico looked up. In the light of the full moon, the rock appeared ancient, yet new. Solid, yet worn.

Majestic, yet ominous.

As the ship made its way through the choppy waters, Nico

marveled at the huge promontory overhead. It stood as a mighty sentinel, keeping watch over all vessels passing through.

Just as I keep watch over you.

At the sound of the Lord's voice, Nico's heart stirred. "Yes, Lord. Thank You for keeping watch over me." He closed his eyes. "And please keep watch over Sofia, too."

Night and day, her face hovered before Nico. Hardly a moment passed by that she did not fill his every thought.

He sighed. He could not be with her soon enough.

A strong gust of wind whipped across Nico's face. He lifted his coat collar and pressed it against his neck, all the while keeping his eyes on the huge rock before him as it passed out of view.

Having passed Gibraltar, the *Perugia* now entered the full, expansive waters of the Atlantic. For the next two-and-a-half weeks, Nico would see only sky and water. Sky and water.

Sky and water.

The earth was big.

But I am far bigger.

"Yes, Lord. You are far bigger. Bigger than any created thing. Bigger than any problem.

"Bigger, even, than my fear of telling Mama and Luca of my decision to move back to Sicily."

Nico shivered and took a deep breath.

The first hint of dawn peeked over the horizon, reminding him that he needed to get some sleep.

Making his way down to the steerage section, he found his bunk above Mama's and fell into it, suddenly exhausted.

In an instant, he was fast asleep.

Chapter Fifteen

The day was cold and cloudy when the *Perugia* sailed past the Statue of Liberty and docked in New York Harbor. Maria watched from the ship's railing, thankful that this time, she would not have to go through the rigorous Ellis Island inspection and examinations. What an ordeal that had been! One she wished upon no one.

A cold wind whipped across the deck, spraying her face with salt water. She wiped the droplets away with her gloved hand. Although spring had raised her lovely head in Sicily, it would be several more weeks before the season arrived in Brooklyn.

Maria searched the wharf for Luca and the children, but the crowds of people waiting for loved ones made it difficult to spot individual faces. "Nico, let's start moving toward the gangplank. Otherwise, we will be overwhelmed by the disembarking crowds."

Nico picked up their two suitcases. "I'll follow you, Mama."

Taking the small basket her sister had given her, now empty except for some dried fruit, Maria headed toward the gangplank. Already several passengers waited there for the ship to come to a full stop. She and Nico found a spot among them.

"Are you glad to be home, son?"

"Only because I've missed Papa, Valeria, and Anna."

"Is that the only reason?"

"Can we talk about this later, Mama? I think it will take more time than we have right now."

"Very well." So the emotional and psychological conflict of

immigrants extended even to their children. As soon as they had time to talk without interruption, she would discuss this with Nico.

Once the ship came to a full stop and the gangplank was lowered, passengers began leaving in droves, their faces solemn with concern about what awaited them in the New World. Most of them were ushered toward the waiting ferries that would take them to Ellis Island.

Maria shuddered. Eight years earlier, she'd been among them. Weary. Worried.

And afraid she wouldn't pass the physical and mental examinations.

She whispered a prayer for her compatriots before taking Nico's arm to search the crowd for Luca and the children. Upon seeing them, her heart warmed.

Luca, Valeria, and Anna greeted Maria and Nico with great joy. Luca opened his arms wide to receive her.

Maria rushed into them, a flood of tears falling from her eyes and moistening his woolen scarf. "Oh, Luca! I missed you so terribly! How good it is to be with you again!"

Luca smothered her face with kisses. "Welcome home, *Cara Mia*! Welcome home!"

Her heart sank. Except for Luca and the children, it didn't feel like home. Home was the country she'd left three weeks earlier. The place where she'd grown up.

The land of her roots.

America seemed like a foreign land. Even after several years of living here.

Would she ever be able to embrace this country as her own?

She squeezed Luca's hand and managed a smile. "How have you been? And the children?"

"We've been as well as can be expected without you. I won't say it's been easy."

She laughed. "You'd better not say that. If you do, I'll turn around and board the ship again and head straight back to Sicily." Did he realize she was only half joking?

Anna and Valeria wrapped their arms around Maria and hugged her tightly. In the nearly two months she'd been gone, both of her daughters had grown.

Anna pressed her cheek against Maria's chest. "Oh, Mama! I missed you so badly. I was afraid you would love Sicily so much you would never come back."

Maria tensed. Had Anna read her mind? "But I did come back, my sweet Anna. I could never stay away from you longer than necessary."

Valeria took Maria's hand. "I was afraid you'd get lost at sea, Mama."

Nico tousled Valeria's curly hair and chuckled. "You, Valeria? The one who never worries about anything or anyone?"

Caught in a trap of her own making, Valeria smiled sheepishly. "I guess I don't worry about *almost* anything. Except Mama."

"Well, if you're going to worry about anyone, let it be Mama. She's worth worrying about."

Meant in jest, Nico's words sounded strangely ominous. As though he knew something was going on inside Maria. Had he sensed her reluctance to leave Sicily? Her hesitance to step foot again on American soil?

Her divided heart?

Valeria threw Nico a solid, sisterly rebuttal. "But I never worried about you, Nico."

"Haha! That's because you don't love me as much as you love Mama."

"Should I?"

Maria's heart warmed at the friendly banter between Nico and his sister. It was like old times.

Taking both of her daughters by the hand, she followed Luca and Nico toward the waiting horse and buggy. The day was frigid, with an overcast sky portending snow. Fumes from nearby factories filled the air, rendering it hazy and difficult to breathe. Elm and maple trees—still barren in late February—reflected the barrenness of her heart.

Lord, You have given me so much. A wonderful husband. Three beautiful children. A roof over my head and plenty of food to eat. Help me to be content. She swallowed hard. *Even if I must live far from my homeland.*

Maria and the children piled into the horse and buggy while Luca gave the driver instructions to take them home. Luca then entered and sat beside Maria. Nico, Valeria, and Anna sat on the opposite bench.

Anna was the first to speak. "Mama, *Signora* Addevico fed us royally while you were gone."

Maria smiled. "I'm glad to hear. Since she is a far better cook than I am, it will likely take you a few weeks to re-adjust to your Mama's fare."

Anna's facial expression turned apologetic. "Oh, Mama. You're a great cook!" Anna then looked at Papa with a twinkle in her eye. "But, as for Papa, I think he needs to practice a little more."

Everyone erupted into laughter. Yes, it was good to be back with her family again. How did the old saying go? *Home is where the heart is.*

But where was home when one's heart was split between two worlds?

* * * *

During Maria's first days back in Brooklyn, the demands of caring for her family overshadowed her intention to talk with Luca about the possibility of returning to their homeland. But the thought still nagged her. Still niggled at her brain.

Still kept her up at night.

She'd have to bring it up to Luca soon or forever lay it to rest. It wasn't fair to keep her sisters waiting for her decision about *Bella Terra*. They didn't have the financial resources to keep the farm afloat much longer, if at all.

Tonight would be as good a time as ever to bring up the topic to Luca. Nico would be working late, and Valeria and Anna would be spending the evening playing board games with their friend Lia at Enza Addevico's apartment down the hall.

"Would you like another cup of espresso?" Maria stood at the kitchen sink, drying the last dish on the rack, while Luca sat at the kitchen table, reading *Il Progresso Italo-Americano*.

Luca lifted his head from the newspaper and smiled. "Yes. I would. Then we can sit and catch up on each other's lives."

Maria nodded. "I'd like that very much." Lately, they hadn't done much catching up on anything, so busy had their lives become. With Luca gone for days at a time at his job on the railroad, she'd been left to herself a good deal. Nico worked long days at the clothing factory, and Valeria and Anna spent most of the day at school. To fill her days and earn extra income, Maria had resumed taking in some sewing. But sewing at home was lonely work.

Maria poured two demitasse cups of espresso and brought them to the kitchen table. The familiar aroma of the steaming brew rose to her nostrils, bringing back vivid memories of laughing with Mama over a cup of espresso at their kitchen table in *Bella Terra*. She choked back the sudden sob that formed in her throat. Now would be a good time to bring up the topic of moving back to Sicily. Luca was in the mood to listen.

She sat down across from her husband. At forty-seven, his handsome face already showed signs of aging. Silver strands now streaked his once-sandy-colored hair. His eyes, once bright with blue light, had now grown dull with the weariness and fatigue of hard labor on the railroad. Life in America had taken a huge physical and emotional toll on him. At this rate, he'd be an old man by the time he was fifty.

Maria reached for his hand. "Luca, I want to talk with you about something."

"Of course." He stroked each finger on her hand, waiting for her to speak.

Maria hesitated. "It's very important. It might upset you, so please hear me out."

Luca furrowed his brows, his eyes revealing concern at what Maria was about to say. "I promise I will."

Maria released his hand and took a sip of espresso. "Returning to Sicily for Mama's funeral had a profound impact on me." She studied his eyes. "I was glad I arrived in time to spend Mama's last days with her. But I was deeply grieved that she died not long after I arrived."

Luca's gaze was glued to hers, encouraging her to continue.

"But the biggest impact on me was being back in Sicily. It felt so right, Luca. So natural."

Her eyes pleaded with him. "So where I belong."

She stopped, waiting for his reply. Hoping he'd read between the lines.

Hoping he'd read her heart.

"What are you saying to me, Maria?" His voice sounded impatient. Annoyed.

Almost threatening.

She stiffened. "I'm saying, would you consider moving back?"

Without saying a word, Luca rose from the table, shoved his hands into his pockets, and walked toward the balcony door. A shaft of sunlight streamed through the glass pane and ribboned across the distressed wooden floor, stopping at Maria's feet.

She kept her gaze on her husband.

His back toward her, he stared outside for what seemed like an eternity. Then he turned, walked back to the table, and sat down.

Maria's heart pounded like a thousand drums under an African sky. Every muscle in her body tensed as she waited for Luca's response.

He folded his arms across his chest. "Why do you want to move back to Sicily?"

Why? Could he not see? Was he so blinded by his dream that he'd left reality altogether?

"Luca, what has living here done for us, other than bring us trouble, heartache, and poverty? Where are the streets of gold we heard about? You're breaking your back every day in frigid weather building a cross-country railroad. And what of the children? Nico could have had his own tailoring business in Sicily, but, instead, he's working long hours as an underpaid employee in the garment industry."

Luca gazed into her eyes. "What of God's dream? What of our calling to spread the Gospel here?"

"But are you sure God meant for us to spread the Gospel in America? He knows that Italy needs the Gospel far more than America does. Look at what happened to the Brooklyn Mission. It folded. I'm sure we did some good while it was open, but now there's nothing left of it." She paused. "Do you think God may be telling us our work here is done?"

Luca rubbed his hand across his face. "What of the children? What of their futures?"

"I don't know, Luca. Do you see a future for them here? The girls might end up marrying Americans and lose their Italian heritage altogether. As for Nico, he mentioned to me that he wants to move back to Sicily. Besides, when I was in Italy, my sisters and I discussed the possibility of turning *Bella Terra* into an inn in order to save it. If we did, all of us could work together there."

Luca remained silent for a long time. Maria knew better than to prod him for an answer. Her husband needed to deliberate. To consider all angles of a decision.

To weigh every alternative.

Only then would he make a final decision.

But what if Luca finally decided that they should live out the rest of their lives in Brooklyn?

Maria shuddered at the frightening thought.

Chapter Sixteen

Several weeks had elapsed since Nico's visit. Don Franco made his way from his campus apartment to his classroom across the expansive lawn of the Classical Academy for Boys. The frigid days of late February had given way to the less bitter days of March. But still, winter reigned and would do so for a few more weeks.

Overhead, a pale sun peeked through an overcast gray sky, looking for a place to burst forth. The eaves on the old school buildings had shed their icicles and replaced them with the nests of two white-spotted starlings. Soon, spring would follow closely on the heels of winter in another extravagant display of eternal renewal.

Franco's heart warmed at the memory of Nico's visit. He'd taken his son to Milano, where they'd explored the magnificent Duomo, the splendid Academy of Fine Arts, and the famous Basilica of Sant'Ambrogio. They'd shared a pizza at one of the many *trattorie* lining the picturesque side streets of the city and spent long evening in Franco's apartment, talking about Nico's ancestors and the heritage he'd inherited through his biological father. They'd discussed Nico's budding relationship with Sofia and his desire to return to Sicily to marry her and build a life with her.

Franco had encouraged his son to follow his dream. To marry Sofia.

To settle in Sicily.

But would he?

Franco's plan was to move back to the island himself. Although he enjoyed his work as headmaster of the academy in

Milano, the harsh winters were taking an increasing toll on his aging bones. The milder winters of Sicily beckoned him.

And Nico's return would seal his own decision to go home to Sicily. The pleasant thought of spending his latter years near his son—and near his future grandchildren—filled his soul with joy. Oh, that God would grant him this desire of his heart!

But much hinged on Maria's reaction to their son's decision. What would she think of Nico's desire to return to the land of his birth? To marry Sofia?

To build a relationship with his father, the man who'd brought devastation to her life?

She wouldn't like the idea of being far from her son. Especially if Nico lived close to the man who'd so drastically altered her life.

Franco pushed the heavy thoughts aside. No use trying to draw conclusions before hearing from Nico. The boy had promised to write to him after speaking with Maria and Luca. All that remained was to await Nico's letter.

Franco quickened his pace as the clock in the bell-tower struck nine. As he entered the centuries-old building, students straggled into the classroom for the early-morning philosophy class. Among them was Matteo.

He slowed and waited for Franco. "So, *Professore*, are we going to resume our discussion on the existence of God?"

Franco smiled. "Indeed, we are." He placed a hand on Matteo's shoulder. "Would you like to start off the class with your recent discovery?" Matteo's change of heart following his father's death would provide a powerful testimony to the topic.

The student's eyes welled up with tears. "Yes. I would like that very much."

"Good. After our opening prayer, I will give you the floor."

Matteo nodded. "Thank you, *Professore*. I will do you proud."

"And you will do your father proud as well." A lump

formed in Franco's throat. He was about to hear another example of the ageless story of redemption, a story that continued to transform lives because of the simple yet profound and infinite love of the Savior, Jesus Christ.

It was a story Franco never tired of hearing. A story that had transformed his own life.

A story he would tell until his dying day.

* * * *

Maria cleared the last dish from the dinner table and placed it in the sink. Nearly two weeks had passed since she'd spoken with Luca about moving back to Sicily. She felt the pressure of getting back to her sisters regarding the farm. She'd promised to send them a reply within three months of her return, and they'd agreed to wait. But they couldn't hold out much longer without declaring bankruptcy.

She took the espresso pot from the stove and poured some of the freshly brewed espresso into two demitasse cups, one for herself and one for Luca. Then she brought the cups to the kitchen table and sat down across from her husband.

Luca was engrossed in reading *Il Progresso*. Should she interrupt him? He'd just returned home from several difficult days of working on the railroad. Now might not be the best time to question him again about moving, but she needed a final answer from him.

He looked up from his newspaper and smiled. "Thank you for the coffee."

"You're welcome." His kind and pleasant demeanor prompted her to ask the question that was burning in her heart. "Luca, have you thought any more about our conversation?"

He took a sip of his coffee and leaned back in his chair. "Yes. I've been thinking about it, and I believe God wants us to stay here in Brooklyn."

Maria's heart plummeted to the soles of her feet. "Are you sure, Luca?"

"Yes, I'm sure."

"But it makes no sense!" Her insides roiled.

Luca smiled. "Since when has God ever made sense?"

She had to admit Luca's comment was true. Yet, every fiber of her being rebelled against his decision.

Maria stood. "But what about what I believe?" Fire flared in Maria's belly. "I don't recall your asking me my opinion. This is entirely your decision."

Luca pressed her. "Are you saying you don't support me in my decision?"

She raised her voice. "That's exactly what I'm saying. I don't want to remain here, Luca. I want us to move back to Sicily where we can all be together for the rest of our lives. If Nico moves back, we may never see him again." She lowered her voice. "I also want to save *Bella Terra*. If we don't move back, my sisters will have to sell the farm."

"I know that's very upsetting to you, Maria, but there's nothing I can do about it."

"Indeed, there is. You can take us all back to Sicily to live, and we could save *Bella Terra*."

Luca stood and raked his fingers through his hair. "I'm sorry, Maria, but I just can't do it. I believe we would be disobeying God if we were to move back to Sicily."

"Very well. If that is the case, I may just have to move back there myself!" She couldn't believe she'd spoken the harsh words.

Luca stopped short. "You wouldn't really do that, would you?"

Maria fell into the chair. No, she would never leave Luca. She could never leave Luca. She loved him too much.

But the frightening question was, *Did she love Nico more?*

Chapter Seventeen

The sun slipped below the horizon just as Nico left the clothing factory for the last time. A rush of relief swept over him as he closed the door behind him. Since his and Mama's return from Sicily, they'd both avoided the controversial topic that had created tension between them.

A topic that had to be resolved before his upcoming departure.

Once back in Brooklyn, he'd lost no time preparing for his move back to Sicily. The day after his return, he'd booked passage on a ship scheduled to set sail on April 17th, leaving him approximately six weeks to tie up loose ends before his departure. He'd tell Mama and Luca of his plans at a later date. No use troubling them more than necessary. Learning of his decision to move back to Sicily would be shock enough to them. Who knew what they would do if he told them he'd already booked passage?

After purchasing his one-way ticket, he'd then made arrangements to speak with his foreman regarding leaving his job at the garment factory. He wanted to give his boss at least a month's notice, although hiring a replacement would be an easy task. With so many immigrants looking for work, Nico's job would be filled quickly and without challenge. He was sure of it. He'd also sorted through his clothing and belongings for items he would no longer need—items he would donate to his church.

A cluster of yellow daffodils lined the sidewalk, signaling the welcome arrival of spring. Nico's heart soared. Having officially resigned from his job shortly after his return from

Sicily, he'd spent the last few weeks training his replacement. His boss had been understanding but disappointed, citing Nico as one of his best workers to date. At least he was leaving a good legacy behind him. And he would forge an even better one in Sicily.

In a few moments, he reached the train station and boarded the elevated train that would take him home from work for the last time. Weary workers sat solemnly in wooden seats, immersed in their own thoughts. One leaned against the window, snoring loudly in deep sleep. A few others buried their heads in the evening newspaper, while still others stared into space, oblivious to their surroundings.

Nico found a seat by the window. Excitement filled his soul. And with it a growing sense of freedom. Not just the freedom of moving back to his homeland and, especially, to Sofia. But something deeper. A sense of freedom at finally making his own decisions for his life. Of breaking free from what had become Mama's stifling possessiveness.

Her oppressive control.

For whatever reason, until his visit to Sicily, he'd been reluctant to admit to himself that Mama had kept him under her thumb. Perhaps he'd been afraid of disrespecting her. Or of thinking of her in a bad light. But truth be told, over the years, she'd hovered over him like a hawk, intruding into his life in a way that was unhealthful for both of them.

Destructive, even.

To his surprise, he'd begun to resent Mama's attempts to plan his life for him. Yes, she was his mother. But she didn't own him. Nor did she know everything about him. Some parts of him were his own to figure out. His own to understand and determine.

Like his decision to marry Sofia.

Nico inhaled a long breath. How to make Mama understand that he was now a grown man, capable of making his own choices for his life?

He leaned sideways in his seat as the train turned a bend on the tracks. Now that he'd quit his job, purchased his ticket, and cleared out his belongings, there remained only his dreaded conversation with Mama and Luca. A conversation he could no longer put off.

A conversation he'd initiate this weekend.

The evening air was brisk as he exited the elevated train that, for the past two years, had taken him from home to the Manhattan garment district and back again each morning and evening. He'd gotten to know some of his fellow travelers who rode the same train to their respective jobs. He'd also become acquainted with some of the conductors, one of whom hailed from Nico's own province in Sicily.

As the train pulled away, the acrid smell of coal fumes burned his nostrils, provoking a sneeze. He turned aside to avert the disgusted look of a well-dressed businessman in his path.

A look he'd witnessed far too often.

The loud grating of the train's wheels against the track jolted Nico's already taut nerves. He made his way down the steps onto the busy street.

Dark settled over Brooklyn as he began his walk to his tenement house. A cool breeze brushed across his face. Thank God this was the last time he'd have to make this trip.

He wended his way through the side streets that led to Brooklyn's center. Piles of trash stood like sentinels along the curb, awaiting pickup. Young boys selling newspapers paced the sidewalks, peddling the day's latest news. Nico purchased a newspaper from one of them.

This weekend would be Luca's last before leaving Monday morning for his next week-long assignment working on the Pennsylvania Railroad. For days Nico had been rehearsing his conversation with Mama and Luca. He'd begin by telling them of his love for them and his gratitude for all they'd done for him. Then he'd tell them of his love for Sofia and of his desire to marry her. He'd then explain his growing desire to return to his roots, to get to know Don Franco better, a desire fanned into a flame by his recent visit to Sicily with Mama. Finally, he'd explain he'd do his best to help save *Bella Terra* from being sold. Although he could see no way of doing so, his interest might at least get Mama on his good side regarding returning to Sicily and give her some sense of resigned comfort.

He rounded the next corner. Brooklyn's main street teemed with people returning home from work. A streetcar chugged by, bulging with passengers headed to Manhattan.

Looking carefully both ways, he crossed the street to the other side, deftly avoiding the horse-drawn buggies and carriages making their way through the city proper. A horse nearly nipped his coat as he passed in front of it. Nico dodged him just in time to avoid being knocked over by the startled animal.

As he turned the corner onto the street where his tenement house was located, a lone, stray dog greeted him, wearily wagging his tail. Nico reached down to pet the poor animal before turning into his building.

He gritted his teeth. No matter what, he had to go through with this conversation with Mama and Luca. There was no way out of the unpleasant task. Nor could he wait any longer. Sofia awaited him, as did Don Franco.

Most of all, Nico's future beckoned him. A future he hoped would be all he envisioned it to be.

He entered the stairwell and walked up the three flights to his family's flat.

Mama was placing dinner on the table when Nico walked in. "*Ciao*, Mama."

He took off his coat and hung it on the coat rack. He then removed his shoes and placed them on the mat by the front door.

Mama's warm smile encouraged him. "Welcome home!

I've cooked your favorite meal. *Pasta alla marinara.*"

He smiled and walked over to her in his stockinged feet. "You're the best Mama in the entire world." He planted a kiss on her cheek.

"And you're the best son." Mama's voice was full of emotion.

Nico laughed. "You say that only because you have no other sons."

Mama playfully swatted him with a dishtowel. Her jovial mood bode well for their looming conversation.

"What about me, Mama?" Anna chimed in. "Am I the best daughter in the entire world?"

"That's not fair!" Valeria was quick to retort. "You have two daughters, Mama. Both of us can't be the best."

"Indeed, both of you can be."

"But that's illogical." Valeria was adamant.

Maria placed a large bowl of pasta on the table. "Actually, it is very logical. You see, each person created by God is a unique masterpiece that cannot be compared to any other person. Therefore, each of my daughters is the best daughter in her uniqueness."

Nico chuckled. "I must say, Mama, you are quite the diplomat. You should run for political office."

Mama laughed. "Thank you for the compliment. I just might consider doing that one day. How was work today?"

"Busy and productive." He would wait until later to tell her it was his last day on the job. No sense destroying the happy atmosphere unnecessarily.

Anna approached him. "Aren't 'busy' and 'productive' synonyms?"

Nico tousled his youngest sister's hair. "Actually, no. One can be busy without being productive."

Anna grinned at her sister. "Just like Valeria!"

Valeria made a sour face at her sister.

The friendly family banter continued for a few moments more. Nico was relieved Mama was in a good mood. It would make his conversation with her and Luca easier. At least, he hoped so.

Just then Luca entered through the front door. "I'm home."

"Papa! Papa!" Anna ran toward Luca and gave him a bear hug. "I'm so glad you're home."

Luca gave her a hug. "I am, too, my little one."

"I'm not little, Papa! I'm ten years old."

Luca feigned surprise. "Excuse me for my gross miscalculation. I must remember that children grow older while I remain stuck at the same age."

Anna giggled. "Papa, you're silly."

"Dinner's ready." Mama brought the salad to the table.

Nico's tension evaporated amid the jovial banter. Perhaps his conversation with Mama and Luca wouldn't be as difficult as he'd imagined.

* * * *

The next morning, after his sisters had left to play with Enza's daughter, Nico approached Luca and Mama. "Do both of you have a few moments to talk with me?" His heart pounded. Why was he so afraid? Surely he was making the proverbial mountain out of a molehill.

"Of course." Mama was the first to speak. "What is it, *figlio mio?*"

Luca nodded in agreement. "Yes. What is it, son?"

Nico took a chair at the kitchen table and sat directly across from Mama and Luca. He studied their faces before proceeding, trying to gauge how best to begin. "There's something I must tell you. But I want to prepare you first by stating that I don't think you are going to like what I am about to say."

Mama's countenance fell, but she remained silent.

He drew in a deep breath to steady his nerves. "Mama, while we were in Sicily, you told me the truth about my birth father. To say I was stunned by the rape would be an understatement, but I was not completely surprised at the revelation that Don Franco is my biological father. For the past few years, I've noticed I resemble him." Nico read the discomfort on Mama's face. "When I finally saw him again at *Nonna's* funeral, my suspicions about our resemblance were confirmed." He lowered his voice. "And when you, Mama, told me the truth about Franco, I found myself relieved."

Mama arched an eyebrow. "Why relieved?"

"Because I finally knew the truth about who I am. The truth you spoke to me and the time I spent with Don Franco fulfilled a deep-seated need of mine. You introduced me to my birth father, and he introduced me to my roots—something I've wanted to discover for a long while now."

Luca intervened. "But why, Nico? Why this obsessive need to discover who you are? Isn't it enough to know you are our son and we love you?"

Nico paused, hesitant to continue. But continue he must. "To be honest with you, it is not enough."

Mama looked puzzled. "But are you not happy, my son?"

"It's not that I'm not happy, Mama. It's that I had to resolve the issue of where I came from before I could move forward with my life."

Luca leaned forward. "And so, now that you've resolved that issue, can you not just continue with your life as it has been?"

Nico shook his head and took in a deep breath. "No. Now that I know who I am, I've made a major decision." The time had come for him to break the news to them. "I've decided to return to Sicily and marry Sofia."

Mama's eyes turned to fire. "I told you I forbid it!"

"Mama, please hear me out."

Mama stood and began pacing the floor. "There is nothing to hear. The matter is closed, and I refuse to have you reopen it."

Luca raised a palm in protest. "Maria, please listen to what the boy has to say. Please show him your respect."

"Show him *my* respect? What about *his* respect for me? I'm only his mother. I'm only the woman who brought him into this world and raised him for the last nineteen years. Does that mean nothing?"

Nico's heart sank to his feet. His hopes that the conversation would go well had suddenly been destroyed. "Mama, please. Allow me to explain my heart."

"You have no heart! Any son who wants to leave his mother after all she's done for him is heartless."

Nico swallowed hard. What had happened to Mama? Never had she treated him so harshly. She was not the same person he'd grown up with. What was going on?

"Maria, please!" Luca insisted. "Give the boy a chance to speak."

"Very well. But what he says had better be—"

"What you want it to be?" Luca's voice was unusually stern.

Mama's face contorted. "Are you insinuating I'm being unfair?"

"Yes, I think you are being grossly unfair. Allow Nico the opportunity to explain his reasons for wanting to return to Sicily and marry Sofia."

Nico's soul teetered on the edge of despair. What he'd intended to be a time of sharing his heart had turned into a major war. "Mama, I'm sorry. I did not intend to cause you such anguish. Please, I beg of you, give me a few moments to explain what's going on inside me." He closed his eyes, smarting with incipient tears, and rubbed them.

Mama sat down again, folded her hands, and placed them on her lap. "I won't interrupt you. I will hear you out to the end."

"Thank you, Mama." In her eyes he read sorrow, anguish, and fear.

True to her word, Mama remained silent while Nico proceeded to explain. "Mama, first of all, know that I love you deeply and that I will always love you. You gave me life, and I will be forever grateful to you for that."

Mama's face softened.

"Our recent visit to Sicily changed my life. Changed it in ways I'd never imagined. When we left Brooklyn, I had every intention of making my life here in America, although, I must confess, I had been thinking about returning to Sicily because of some questions I had about who I really am."

Mama raised an eyebrow.

"You see, since I knew Luca is not my biological father, I'd begun to wonder who was. I was afraid to say anything to you because you'd never spoken about the situation to me, other than to tell me you had forgiven Don Franco for something. But you never told me what that 'something' was." Nico paused, giving Mama and Luca time to digest what he was saying. "When you finally told me the truth about my birth, part of me was stunned, while part of me was not. Actually, part of me was happy I now knew the truth and could move forward from there."

Mama's eyes filled with tears.

Nico glanced at Luca. His gaze upon Nico was steady and compassionate.

"The time I spent with Don Franco in Milano was priceless. I know you weren't too happy about my going, Mama, but I had to go. And I'm so glad I did. I saw firsthand how God can change a repentant heart and make it like Christ's. I also learned so much about my lineage and from whom I descend.

And I was able to relate to Don Franco as my biological father and not just as a teacher and farmhand." Nico paused. "Can you understand that, Mama?"

Mama nodded.

Nico still had not addressed the issue of Sofia, perhaps the more pressing of the two issues he needed to discuss with Mama and Luca. "As for Sofia...."

Mama squared her jaw and shifted in her chair but spoke not a word.

"When I first met Sofia, I was struck by her beauty. But more than that, I was struck by her soul. Her quiet demeanor. There was something special about her. Something that connected with me on a very deep level." Nico nervously studied Mama's face. What was she thinking?

Mama answered his thoughts. "And that is reason enough to want to marry her?"

"Mama, meeting Sofia was like being punched in the stomach with a force bigger than myself. I was smitten. Instantly smitten. Can you understand that? I've fallen in love with her, Mama."

"Nonsense! What do you know about falling in love? You're only nineteen years old."

Mama's words pierced Nico's heart. His muscles tensed. "I think a man knows when he's in love, Mama."

"A man, yes. But you are only a boy."

Fire rose in Nico's belly. He'd never disrespected Mama before, and he wasn't about to disrespect her now. But he must make his case clear. "Mama, please look at the situation from my perspective. I am now a grown man. I can make my own decisions. Yes, I will seek your advice when necessary, but I will not always follow it. And as much as you may not like that, I must ask that you respect this fact."

"So, we have come to a battle of the wills, have we?"

Luca raised a palm in mid-air. "Maria, please. What Nico

164

is saying is true. He is no longer a child. We must respect him as a young man and allow him to make his own decisions."

At least Luca understood him. But he needed Mama to understand him as well.

"Mama, please hear what I'm saying. I am in love with Sofia, and I am going to marry her."

Maria stopped him short. "I said I forbid it!"

What had happened to Mama? To the kind, tenderhearted, understanding woman in whose steadfast love he'd grown up?

"Maria, please allow Nico to finish."

"No! I've heard enough. Nico is my son, and he must do what I say!"

Nico's stomach ached. "But, Mama, with all due respect, I have made up my mind."

Mama stood. "But, *figlio mio*, you hardly know her. You met her only one time, at *Nonna's* funeral."

"Actually, Mama, I visited her on my way home from Milano."

Mama gasped. "And you didn't tell me?"

"I didn't think it was necessary to tell you."

"Oh, so now you're keeping things from your Mama. Since when don't you tell me everything?"

"Maria, Nico is right. You cannot hover over his every move."

Nico's stomach sank to the pits of despair. He'd planted his foot on a land mine, and the mine had now exploded. "Mama, please put yourself in my shoes."

Mama leaned a hand on the table in front of him. "I've been doing that all of my life, Nico. Every minute of every day, I've been doing my best to protect you, to keep you from harm, to guide you in the right path. And this is what I get for my efforts?"

"Mama, I'm grateful for all you've done for me, but at some point, I must do for myself."

Mama planted her hands on her hips. The veins at her temples bulged. "Very well. I never thought I would have to say this to my own son, but I must say it now. Nico, if you move back to Sicily and marry Sofia, then I can no longer consider you my son."

Nico's knees grew limp as his heart caved in. A sob rose to his throat, but he forced it to remain there. Now was not the time to show weakness. Now was the time to stand strong in his resolve to direct his life as he saw fit.

Now was the time for him finally to be a man. He rose abruptly and moved toward the door.

"Where are you going?" Mama called after him.

"As far away as I can get."

He grabbed hold of the doorknob. "I've booked passage on the *Perugia*. It sails on Monday."

Her heart fell to her feet. "But, Nico! Why so soon?"

"It's not soon enough!"

With that, he left the flat, slamming the door behind him.

Chapter Eighteen

Stunned by Nico's angry and abrupt departure, Maria stood immobile in the tiny flat. Her son's uncharacteristic behavior had shocked her. Unnerved her.

Crushed her.

Never in his entire life had he acted in such a hurtful manner. Never had he shouted at her.

Never had he slammed a door in her face.

For her usually calm, even-keeled son to do so now meant only one thing: he'd reached the limits of her control over his life. He'd passed the point of no return.

The bands tying him to her had snapped, and he'd broken free.

A shiver coursed through her veins. She sighed and collapsed into a chair, shaking all over. Nico's last words played over and over again in her mind. *He'd already booked passage on the* Perugia! *He would leave for Sicily on Monday!*

In only two short days!

How could this be? How could the precious son of her womb, who had always been the delight of her heart, do such a thing to her? What had possessed him to purchase a one-way ticket to leave for Sicily—and to leave forever—without even mentioning his plans to her? Without even giving her enough time to process his decision?

Without even allowing her enough time to say goodbye?

Her body fell limp. What should she do? What could she say? Tears rose to her eyes. There was nothing left to say. Nico had won this battle, and she must accept her defeat.

Yet, she could not—would not—allow him to leave for

Sicily without first reconciling with him. To separate in anger would be against the Lord's will. She must make things right before he left. Otherwise, her grief would be unbearable.

Her heart pounded against her rib cage, making it difficult for her to breathe. She'd made a mess of things, and now it was too late to go back and retrieve her bitter words.

Too late to un-ring the bell.

Nico's mind was made up. No amount of persuading, cajoling, threatening, or demanding could change it. The only thing left for her to do was to accept his decision to return to Sicily and marry Sofia and put matters into God's hands.

But was that really the only thing left to do?

She leaned her forehead on the palm of her hand. Maybe there was one more thing to do.

Return to Sicily herself.

How else could she continue to be near her son? How else could she continue to share in his life?

How else could she take care of him?

The ugly truth faced her head-on. Yes. She wanted to control her son's life.

The Holy Spirit's correction came swiftly but gently. *You must let Nico go. He does not belong to you. He has never belonged to you. He belongs to Me.*

Maria needed to be alone. To sort out her tormenting feelings.

She took a deep breath. Nico's decision to return to Sicily and to marry Sofia had stirred up old feelings of fear, anger, and resentment within her. Feelings she thought she'd buried long ago. She needed space to sort them out. Time to process them.

Conversation with her heavenly Father to receive His wisdom and His healing love.

"I need to go out for a while."

Luca nodded. "I understand."

Grabbing her coat and an umbrella from the coat rack, she

left the apartment and headed toward the park.

What had started as a light rain had turned into a down-pour. Maria walked briskly down Fulton Street, past the post office and the *Daily Eagle* building. All around her, people rushed to find refuge from the rain. Mothers with young children in tow hastened into nearby stores, seeking shelter. Taxicabs honked as they wove their way between horse-driven carriages that moved at a snail's pace. Businessmen in raincoats and carrying leather briefcases ducked into the lobbies of tall buildings, waiting for the rain to subside.

The wind tugged at Maria's umbrella, making it difficult for her to hold it steady.

Just like her heart.

Nico's decision to marry Sofia and return to Sicily had blindsided her. Thrown her off her feet.

Ripped the very heart right out of her.

She tilted the umbrella to avoid its turning inside out.

A pedestrian bumped into her. "So sorry, ma'am!" He hastened by before she could offer her own apology.

Maria angled her umbrella so she could see more than the sidewalk beneath her. Rain water rushed down drainage pipes lining the buildings and then covered the sidewalk, forming puddles. She barely averted stepping into one of them.

Her tears mingled with the falling rain. Never in her wildest dreams had she expected that Nico would fall in love with a girl living in Sicily. That he would want to return to the land of his birth.

That he would betray his mama.

Yes, that's what it felt like. A betrayal. But why? Nico was an adult now. Free to make his own choices. If he wanted to move back to Sicily, what was it to her? If he wanted to marry Sofia, who was Maria to object?

Just as quickly as it had started, the rain stopped, making way for a sliver of sunlight that burst through the clouds. Maria drew a deep breath.

She'd nearly reached the small park that beckoned her ahead, offering some privacy from the city noise.

Closing her umbrella, she entered the park and found a small bench at the far end. She withdrew a handkerchief from her coat pocket, wiped the bench dry, and then sat down.

Nearby, a small fountain bubbled gently, instantly soothing her troubled soul. Around the fountain, yellow daffodils swayed in the light wind, reminding her that spring was here. The season when God makes all things new.

Would He make her emotions new? Her perceptions? Her thinking?

She inhaled a deep breath of rain-cleansed air and then rested her umbrella against the bench. If she were honest with herself, she had to ask why Nico's decision to return to Sicily bothered her so much. Was it that she would miss him terribly? Yes. That certainly was a huge part of it.

But there was something more. Something she didn't want to admit to herself.

Something she was ashamed of.

She was jealous. Jealous that her son had given his heart to another woman. No longer would Maria be the most beloved woman in his life. Jealous that Nico would have the joy of living out his life in Sicily, the island that had witnessed her birth and her upbringing.

Maria's skin bristled. She tried to quiet her soul to hear the voice of God, but the raging emotional storm within her drowned it out.

An elderly woman walking with a cane shuffled toward the bench. "Do you mind if I rest here for a moment?" The woman smiled. "These legs have seen better days." Wisps of thin white hair peeked out from a bright yellow scarf she wore over her head. Her brown woolen coat, frayed at the cuffs, reached to the ground, covering heavy black boots.

Although Maria had hoped to be alone with the Lord, she could not refuse the humble request of the old woman. "Not at all." Maria slid over toward the edge of the bench to allow room for the woman to sit down.

"I hope I'm not disturbing you." The woman heaved a great sigh as she settled her robust body onto the bench. "I'd gone out to the post office to mail a letter to my daughter and got caught in the horrendous downpour." She placed her cane across her lap and held it tightly with both hands. "Glad the sun is out again. No telling if I would have made it home in the rain."

It was one thing for the woman to sit down. It was quite another for her to engage in conversation. Perhaps Maria should find a quieter spot to pray and listen to God.

The woman turned toward her. Her eyes, framed by tiny lines, twinkled with joy. "Did you get caught in the rain, too?"

Maria smiled in spite of herself. "Yes. It was only drizzling when I left home."

The woman leaned back on the bench, closed her eyes, and smiled. "God is good to send us rain. What would we do without it?" She opened her eyes and pointed a gnarled finger at Maria. "Oh, we may not like the rain, especially like today, when we get caught in it." The woman chuckled. "But do you know that rain reminds me of the trials of life? They sometimes come in a downpour but are meant to produce patience in us. But refreshing always follows the rain." She closed her eyes again. "Yes. Always focus on the refreshing after the rain."

Maria pondered the old woman's words. *Refreshing after the rain*. That was an interesting perspective. Maria hadn't considered trials in that way.

"You are a wise woman."

The old woman laughed. "I've been called many things in my lifetime, but never 'wise.'"

"What made you so?"

"Do you mean old or wise?"

Maria laughed. "Wise."

"Time made me old, but trials made me wise." She placed a hand on Maria's arm and chuckled. "Believe me, *wise* is better than *old*." She broke into a hearty laugh that filled the park bench with life.

"Well, I've interrupted you long enough. I shall now resume my walk home."

Maria had a sudden urge to stop the woman from leaving. "Please. Tell me your name. Mine is Maria."

"And mine is Eva."

"Can we be friends, Eva?"

"I would like that very much. But, perhaps, that is something you should ask of the Lord during your time with Him here in the park."

A chill scurried over Maria's skin. How did the woman know she had come to the park to spend time with the Lord?

"Where do you live?"

The woman looked at Maria, her gaze seeing something far beyond. She smiled. "I live in the secret place of the Most High God."

A chill coursed through Maria's veins. Scripture spoke of entertaining angels unawares. Was Eva an angel?

Eva removed her cane from her lap and placed it solidly in the ground in front of her. Then, leaning carefully on the cane, she hoisted herself up from the bench and sighed. "Thank the Lord for canes." She smiled at Maria. "It is good always to give thanks to the Lord." A supernatural love emanated from Eva's eyes. "Always remember. Trials precede refreshing. Therefore, you can rejoice in your trials."

As Eva turned to leave, a full sun burst forth through the clouds. Its rays covered her and followed her until she reached the edge of the park.

Maria's gaze lost the old woman as Eva's bent figure blended into the city crowds.

* * * *

After the opening prayer, Don Franco gave Matteo the floor.

The boy nodded in thanks. The deep and pensive look on his face revealed to Franco that the death of the boy's father had transformed the young man's usually flippant attitude into a sober one.

A good thing.

All eyes were on Matteo as he approached the front of the classroom. The normally garrulous students were silent as their classmate took the floor.

"Good morning, class." Matteo smiled. "First of all, I would like to thank *Professore* Malbone for allowing me the floor." He nodded toward Franco and then turned back toward the class.

His classmates eyed him warily.

"I wish to speak on a matter that has become very dear to my heart. The matter of the afterlife."

Snickers reverberated throughout the room. These students had known Matteo for a long time. They'd gone through school together. They'd played sports together. And they'd joined him in mocking Franco about his belief in life after death. For all they knew, their compatriot Matteo was about to take his ridicule to a new level.

Matteo lifted his chin, squaring his jaw. "My fellow students, I understand your snickers. Only a short while ago, I sat among you and joined you in the snickering." He cleared his throat. "Much to my dismay. But since then, I have learned that I was wrong in doing so. Wrong to criticize, ridicule, and mock what I have since discovered is the truth." He turned again toward Franco." I want, first of all, to apologize to Don Franco, our distinguished professor, for my abominable behavior toward him. He spoke truth, but I, in my ignorance, belittled him and belittled truth. *Professore*, I am sorry." Matteo then turned again toward his classmates. "Second, I want to apologize to you, my classmates, for fearing you more than fearing God. Only a fool does such a thing, and I have been a fool."

The snickering stopped. In its place, a pall of thick silence fell over the room as students exchanged glances that questioned whether Matteo was serious.

Franco's heart stirred at what God was doing in their midst.

Matteo continued. "Most of you know that my father died a short while ago." Matteo's voice hitched as tears sprang to his eyes. "My father was a fairly young and vibrant man. Only fifty-three years old. Far too young to die. No one expected him to die for a long while yet. He was energetic. Enthusiastic about life. Compassionate. My father was also a godly man who lived his life with reverence toward God." Matteo lowered his eyes. "Unfortunately, I did not follow in his footsteps." He looked up. "Until now." His voice grew strong.

The snickering had ceased. All eyes were glued to him.

"You ask what changed my perspective? Simple. It was my deep love for my father. A love I did not fully recognize nor fully value until he died. It has been said that we do not grasp the full measure of what we have until we lose it. That is how I feel about my father. I did not realize the treasure I had in him.

"Now that I've lost him, I am keenly aware of what I lost. I long to see him again. To embrace him again. To laugh with him again. To eat with him again. To agree to his request that I pray with him." Matteo's voice cracked as tears rolled down his face. "A request I refused again and again."

The young man composed himself. "You see, my father often asked me to pray with him, but I ridiculed and rejected him instead. I told him I was too intellectual for prayer. I told him prayer was for weaklings and God was a crutch used by the weak, by those who were intellectually deficient."

Matteo looked at his classmates and shook his head. His

voice caught. "But I was wrong. Oh, so very wrong."

He took a deep breath. "My father never berated me for my position. He just listened—and loved me. Yes. Always loved me." Matteo paused as a sob escaped from his lips.

Franco sensed the presence of God in a powerful way upon his classroom. He prayed as Matteo resumed.

"You see, my fellow classmates, it takes more faith to believe that God does not exist than it does to believe that He does. Indeed, logic demands that God exist." Matteo's voice grew powerful. Intense. Oratorical. "All that we see around us—the sun, the moon, the stars, the oceans and seas, the animals and trees—indeed, even man himself—all this had to have had a creator. To say something came into being by chance is tantamount to saying this building built itself and is here by chance.

"In the depths of our hearts, we know this is ridiculous. We know we have a creator and our creator is God." He pounded his fist on the podium. "We know this truth!"

He paused. "My father is now with God. I know that with every fiber of my being. My father knew there was a life after this one, and although he tried to convince me of it, I never believed him. But now I do."

He hesitated, as though deciding how to proceed. "After my father died, a strange thing happened. I ran out to the fields near my house and screamed at God. I blamed God for taking my father from me. As I was screaming at God, I suddenly stopped short. Why was I screaming at a God whose existence I refused to acknowledge? Why did I blame my father's death on a God who did not exist? I was an atheist, after all. So, why did my first instinct of deep grief turn to a God who wasn't there?

"The question stopped me short. Did I address God because there is something in man that instinctively knows there is a God who created him? Why did I cry out to God?

"As if those questions did not shake me enough, I fell on

my face in the field. As I wept bitterly, a strange light surrounded me. It was not sunlight, although the sun was shining that day. It was a light that came from another source.

"At first, the light frightened me. But then it roused my curiosity. I lifted my head and felt a peace unlike anything I had ever known. Then, in my heart, I heard the words, 'Your father is now with Me. I want you to be with Me as well. Only believe.'

"Suddenly I knew there was a God. I replied, 'Lord, I believe!'

"As I got up, the light disappeared from around me. But the Light was now within me. I was not the same person who had left the house a short while before. I was a new creature. And I knew it."

Franco stood by as Matteo remained silent for a moment, allowing his message to sink into the hearts of his fellow students.

When Matteo resumed, his voice was clear and powerful. "I urge all of you today to reconsider your beliefs. Ask God to show you for yourself that He does, indeed, exist. Logic itself rebels against the teaching that man happened by chance. If we are honest with ourselves, we will have to admit that such teaching is sheer nonsense."

Matteo turned toward Don Franco. "I have finished, *Professore*. Thank you."

Don Franco nodded. "Thank you, Matteo. Your father would be very proud of you."

Tears glistened in Matteo's eyes. "Thank you."

As Matteo returned to his seat, Franco moved toward the front of the classroom. "My dear students, Matteo has spoken the truth. I pray you take it to heart. You will make many decisions in life, but there is one decision that is, without doubt, the most important one you will ever make. That is the decision you make about Jesus Christ. Jesus Himself asked this question of the Apostle Peter when Jesus said, 'Who do you say that I am?' Peter replied, 'You are the Christ, the Son of the Living God.' Peter recognized the truth about the divinity of God. Matteo has come to recognize that truth as well. Now I leave it to the rest of you to ponder this truth and to embrace it.

"Such a decision begins with a belief that God exists. Matteo has eloquently shown you that faith in God is a matter of the heart first. Once the heart grasps the truth of God's existence, the mind will follow. So, I urge you today to ponder the truth of God's existence and the profound decision that truth requires of us. Then, before it is too late, make that decision in your own life." Franco paused. "Class is dismissed."

Without a word, the students rose and left the classroom. All except Matteo.

Franco turned to him. "Matteo, I am so very proud of you for proclaiming truth. May the truth of the Gospel always be your guiding light. And may you carry that light to all who cross your path."

"Thank you, *Professore*. And thank you for being such a wonderful example to me."

That he who had once been a great sinner should now be an example of God's love humbled Franco.

His gaze followed Matteo as he left the classroom.

Chapter Nineteen

Hands shoved into his pockets, Nico walked down the sidewalk of the narrow street that led to the Brooklyn Christian Center, the church where he and his family had worshipped since their arrival in America eight years earlier. The day was cold and rainy, only adding to the coldness in his heart.

Too bad he'd neglected to bring his umbrella.

Guilt ate at his insides. What had gotten into him? He'd been terribly unkind to Mama. He'd spoken words he never thought would cross his lips. He'd displayed an attitude that was totally inappropriate for a son to display toward his mother.

He released a long breath of air. He'd failed to walk in the love in which the Lord commanded him to walk and stooped to the sin he wanted with all his heart to avoid.

Guilt filled his soul. He'd never spoken to Mama in that harsh tone of voice. Never shouted at her.

Never slammed a door in her face.

What was happening to him?

Was he becoming a rebellious son? Or was he simply asserting an independence that a grown man rightly deserved?

Yes, a grown man. He was now a grown man. Why did Mama have so much trouble accepting that fact? Why did she not see that he wanted to make his own decisions about his life? That he wanted to decide for himself where to live, whom to marry, and what trade to follow?

He wanted—no, he needed—to know if he could make it in life without his Mama hovering over him all the time.

A gust of wind whipped his face. His eyes smarted. A few

more blocks, and he'd reach the church.

He loved the old building, filled each Sunday with fellow believers who eagerly came together to give praise to God. In its small sanctuary, he always found solace for his tired soul. Today he especially needed the comfort the tiny church would offer him.

The church came into view. For the last fifty years, it had stood there, a monument and a testimony to the love and power of God. In those fifty years, many saints had walked through its doors, eager to worship God and to learn of His ways.

As a new immigrant, Nico and his family had been warmly welcomed and accepted by a loving and joyful congregation. Here, he had not tasted at all the prejudice against Italians so rampant in the garment industry and in other facets of society. Instead, in his tiny church, all ethnic groups mingled as one fellowship—Italians, Irish, Poles—united in the same Savior and Lord, Jesus Christ.

Nico climbed the fifteen steps to the front door. He knew there were fifteen because, as a child, he'd counted them every Sunday. For old time's sake, he counted them again. Doing so made his heart both glad and sad. Glad for the good memories. Sad because he would be leaving this wonderful church once and for all.

A lone pigeon perched atop the turret of the old building caught Nico's eye. Where had the creature been? And where was it going? Free to roam the earth at will, the pigeon reflected the longing for freedom in Nico's own heart.

Did God engrave the desire for freedom on the heart of every creature He'd created?

The heavy oaken door creaked loudly as Nico opened it. A gust of wind threatened to send it slamming against the railing. Grabbing the door with both hands, he held it tightly against the wind and then, entering the church, he pulled the door tightly shut behind him.

The sanctuary was empty except for a lone, elderly woman sitting in the front pew.

Nico chose a seat several rows behind her on the opposite side of the sanctuary. A shaft of soft light filtered through a tall, Gothic-style window on the opposite wall. Peaceful silence pervaded the atmosphere.

Nico looked up at the huge wooden cross that hung on the wall behind the altar. Instantly, his heart melted. "O, God, I have sinned against you in the way I treated Mama. Please forgive me. Help me to be the son she needs me to be." He prayed fervently. "And help me to be the husband Sofia deserves."

Sofia. His heart melted at the thought of her. In a few short weeks, he would be with her again. In a few short weeks, he would begin a new life.

In a few short weeks, he would rejoin the man who was his birth father.

But first he must make things right with Mama. He couldn't leave Brooklyn estranged from the woman who'd given him life.

The old woman at the front of the church got up to leave. Shuffling down the aisle, she stopped at his pew and smiled. "Good afternoon."

Nico smiled in return. Strange that she stopped to interrupt him while he was in prayer.

"This is a lovely church. I just stopped by to offer a prayer and must be on my way."

Was the woman in need of help?

Holding on to the pew, she leaned toward Nico. "But first I must convey a message to you from the Lord."

A chill ran through Nico. He waited.

"Be of good cheer. Your destiny awaits you across the seas."

Nico's heart stirred. "May I ask your name?"

The old woman smiled. "My name is Eva."

* * * *

Maria lay immobile, wide awake on the narrow lower bunk she shared with Luca. Night had fallen, and Nico was still not home. Outside the tenement house, the constant barking of a stray dog set her nerves on edge.

Where could Nico be? He'd been gone nearly twelve hours. Never had he stayed out this late before. Worst of all, he'd left angry.

And all because of her.

Her bones turned to ice. Would her son's anger drive him to do something foolish?

The sound of Luca's gentle snoring beside her unnerved her. How could he sleep not knowing where Nico was?

She rose from the bed, trying not to awaken Valeria and Anna in the upper bunk bed. Reaching for her tattered cotton robe that hung on the bedpost, she slipped her arms through the sleeves and then wrapped the robe tightly around her waist before walking to the stove. A cup of *Frutti di Bosco* tea might help soothe her raw nerves.

As she lit the pilot light on the stove, the front door creaked open. She turned abruptly to find Nico walking through the door. Relief flooded her soul.

He closed the door gently behind him. "I didn't think you would still be awake, Mama." His voice was weary and tinged with sadness.

"I couldn't sleep. I was worried about you." She took a deep breath. "Nico, can we talk?"

He nodded. "If you'd like."

She hesitated. "Would you like a cup of *Frutti di Bosco*?"

"That sounds good. It's a bit brisk outside. I could use something hot to break the chill."

As soon as the teapot began to whistle, she turned it off so as not to awaken Luca and the younger children. She took two cups from the cupboard and prepared a cup of tea for Nico and for herself. Into each cup, she stirred a teaspoonful of sugar. Then she brought the tea to the table.

Nico took a chair opposite hers. "Will you forgive me, Mama?"

"Yes, I forgive you, my son." Maria's heart pounded as she faced Nico. "Will you forgive me as well? I have sinned against the Lord and against you."

"Of course, I forgive you, Mama."

Nico took a sip of his tea. "But that doesn't mean you can continue to control me." There was a firm edge to his voice.

She nodded. "You are right. Repentance means to turn away from one's sin and to go in the opposite direction. I want to do that. Truly, I do. But I will need your help."

His gazed was fixed upon her. "Why is letting me go so difficult for you, Mama?"

She took a sip of her tea, mustering the courage to proceed. "I have been afraid, Nico. Ever since I knew I was pregnant with you, I have feared for your safety. Your emotional well-being.

"Your reputation.

"I've wanted to shield you from all hurt." She swallowed hard.

"But, why, Mama? Do you not trust God to take care of me?"

Her son's question pierced her heart. Was he right that she did not really trust God? Her controlling behavior seemed to indicate as much.

Her stomach clenched.

If she were completely honest with herself, she would have to admit her fear reflected a lack of trust in God. In His love for Nico.

And in His love for her.

Did not the Scriptures say God's perfect love casts out fear? If she truly believed God loved her, she would no longer be afraid.

She met Nico's gaze. "If I am honest with myself, I must confess I have not trusted God to take care of you." She lowered her eyes. "I have trusted in my own efforts." She swallowed hard. "And that is idolatry." Hot tears sprang to her eyes. "I'm sorry, Nico." Her voice was a whisper.

Nico rose and put his arms around her.

Suddenly God's grace poured into Maria's heart, bringing with it healing and peace.

She reached for Nico's hand and patted it. "Thank you, my son."

"Mama, I'm glad we spoke. I couldn't bear the thought of leaving for Sicily on bad terms."

"Nor could I. That is the reason I wanted to speak with you now and make things right between us. It would be against the Lord's will for us to remain in strife." She pushed back the lump that rose to her throat. "I will miss you very much, Nico."

"And I you, Mama." He smiled. "But you must come for the wedding."

The wedding. So Nico was really going to marry Sofia. "Yes, we will all come for the wedding. You must let us know when it is."

"As soon as I speak with Sofia, we will set the date, and I will let you know. It will be in late summer, when the weather is warm and the bougainvillea are in full bloom." His face lit up with joy.

Maria's heart lightened. Her son was at peace because he was obeying God's will for his life. And that is all that mattered in the end.

She smiled. "It will be a beautiful wedding."

"I'm going to ask Luca to be my best man."

A rush of joy flooded Maria's heart. "Oh, Nico! Luca will be so honored."

"It is the least I can do for the man who raised me as his own son."

So Nico still considered Luca his papa.

Maria thanked the Lord in the quiet places of her soul.

Nico rose. "And now, I think we'd better get some sleep. Tomorrow will be my last day home before my departure on Monday, and I want to live it to the fullest."

Live it to the fullest. That had always been Nico's way. To live life to the fullest. Perhaps she would do well to take a lesson from him.

Chapter Twenty

The day was cloudy and gray as Maria embraced Nico one last time. Tears streamed down her cheek while her heart broke into a million pieces. Their last day together as a family the day before had been bittersweet for her. They'd gone to church, eaten a special meal she'd cooked for Nico, and then spent the afternoon talking about the future. Maria had helped Nico finish some last-minute packing. Then her son had retired early in preparation for the long sea voyage ahead of him.

Now she, Luca, Valeria, and Anna stood at the pier bidding their final farewells to the beloved son of her heart.

"Take good care of yourself, Nico." Her heart sat precariously on the edge of despair.

"I will, Mama."

"Be sure to eat well, sleep enough, and not overwork." She couldn't help herself. The motherly admonitions rolled off her tongue despite her every effort to the contrary.

Nico chuckled. "Don't worry, Mama. You raised me well. Besides, I will have Sofia to pick up your warnings where you left off."

Though her son had meant the comment to be funny, the thought of her future daughter-in-law's taking her place brought no solace to Maria's heart. Her muscles tensed at the thought of another woman caring for Nico. Yet, she'd promised God to give up control. To trust him with her son.

To let Nico go.

And she intended to keep that promise.

"Besides, Mama, Don Franco will be moving back to Sicily as well."

Maria raised an eyebrow. "Really?" Was this something else Nico had kept from her? "How do you know? Did he tell you as much?"

"When I visited him in Milano, he made reference to the fact that he was thinking of returning to Sicily. Then, last week, I received a letter from him stating that my return was all he needed to make his decision final. He will be meeting me at the Port of Palermo, together with Sofia and her parents."

Why did Maria suddenly feel shut out of Nico's life? No longer needed?

Rejected even?

She swallowed her hurt. And her pride. "I'm glad, Nico. I hope that you learn a lot about yourself from Franco and that you attain the peace you desire about your identity."

"I do, too, Mama."

Luca placed an arm around Nico's shoulders. "I give you my blessing, Nico. Know that I thank God for having given me the opportunity to teach you His ways."

The look on Nico's face told Maria he regretted his earlier words about Luca. "Thank you, *Papa*."

Maria wept as father and son held each other in a tight embrace.

The foghorn blasted in the cool morning air.

"Nico, one more hug! One more hug!" Valeria put her arms around his neck and planted a big kiss on his cheek.

Nico then turned to Anna. His ten-year-old sister wept quietly. He took her into his arms. "I'll ask you to hold down the fort since you are the most level-headed one of the bunch." He forced a laugh through his tears.

Anna grabbed him around the waist. "Oh, Nico. I wish you didn't have to go. But I will be strong because you believe in me."

The foghorn sounded again.

Nico gently withdrew from his little sister's embrace. "It's time to go."

Maria gave him one last hug.

Nico wrapped her in his arms. "I love you, Mama." Tears streamed down his face.

"I love you, too, my precious son." A sob caught in Maria's throat. She would not succumb to it. She would not arouse guilt in her son. She would show happiness for his decision to make his own life by returning to Sicily.

"I will see you all again soon in Sicily. For the wedding." Nico's voice caught. He picked up his knapsack, smiled at Maria, and then headed for the gangplank. The last group of passengers was boarding as the ship's crew master moved to raise the gangplank. Once on board, Nico turned to wave one last time at Maria, Luca, and his sisters before merging into the crowd.

As her son disappeared, Maria's heart shattered. Unable to restrain her anguish any longer, she broke into convulsive sobs. Resting her head on Luca's chest, she cried as the ship pulled out of New York Harbor and set its course toward the great Atlantic Ocean. Toward Sicily.

Toward the end of Maria's dream.

By the time she'd expended all her tears, darkness had settled over Brooklyn. And darkness had settled over her broken heart.

* * * *

Nico stood at the railing of the *Perugia* as it sailed into the Port of Palermo on a lovely afternoon three weeks later. The Mediterranean sun shone brightly over a blue-green sea that shimmered under its warm, comforting rays. Overhead, stratus clouds floated lazily along, in rhythm with the gentle lapping of the waves beneath. Along the dock, seasoned fishermen shouted to one another as they unloaded the day's catch of mackerel, tuna, and squid from their weather-beaten fishing boats. The smell of freshly caught fish mingled with the salty sea air.

It was good to be back in Sicily. Part of him felt as though he'd never left. Although he was only eleven years old when his family had moved to America, he'd spent the greater part of his formative years in this land of his ancestors. His roots lay here, and, now that he was back, he would nourish them and drive them even more deeply into the rich cultural soil of his homeland.

Inhaling a deep and satisfying breath of the fresh salt air, Nico's eyes scanned the crowds of people gathered on the shore, awaiting the arrival of loved ones. Sofia was somewhere among them, with her parents, Teresa and Sergio. Don Franco would be there as well, eagerly awaiting the return of his son.

Nico's heart raced at the prospect of his imminent reunion with Sofia. Hardly a moment had passed that he hadn't thought of her, dreamt of her, longed for her. Although he'd been gone only three months, those three months had seemed like an eternity. He couldn't wait to gaze upon her beautiful face. To be in her presence again.

Not only again, but, this time, for the rest of his life.

A lone seagull swooped down onto the railing in front of him. Was it the same seagull he'd encountered on his trip back to America two months earlier? Perhaps a silly thought. But not for one who was as much in love as he.

As the ship docked, Nico's eyes eagerly scanned the crowds waiting along the pier. Hands waved wildly in the air, seeking to draw the attention of loved ones who had returned. Shouts of Italian first names rose above the chatter, while signs with names scribbled on them rose high above the crowd.

Shading his eyes from the bright sun with his hand, Nico squinted, better to define his gaze. But despite his back-and-forth scanning of the crowd, he could not find Sofia.

Panic unsettled his heart. Had she changed her mind about him?

He quickly brushed aside the ludicrous thought. Disappointed at not finding Sofia, he gathered his belongings and made his way to the front of the line of departing passengers that had begun to form at the end of the gangplank. He wanted to be among the first to disembark.

His heart pounded as he anticipated his longed-for reunion with Sofia. Ever since he'd first met her, she'd consumed his every waking thought. Night and day, he'd dreamt about his return to Sicily, and now that dream was a reality. A dream come true.

A dream about to begin in earnest.

After a few moments, the crew master lowered the gang-plank and the passengers began to disembark.

Once off the ship, Nico searched for Sofia. All around him, families embraced their newly arrived relatives. Tears flowed freely as happy reunions took place on all sides.

But still no sign of Sofia.

Nor of Don Franco.

Nico's pulse quickened. Had they forgotten his arrival date? Had they confused it with another date?

Had they decided not to come?

The crowd began to thin, making his search easier but no more successful. What should he do? He could always make his way to *Bella Terra* on his own. His aunts were expecting him and had wanted to meet him at the dock. But he'd insisted there was no need for them to come, since Sofia would be meeting him. If he hurried, he could make the last train to Ribera and get to *Bella Terra* before nightfall.

Just as Nico decided to leave for *Bella Terra*, Sofia's lyrical voice floated through the air. "Nico, there you are!"

He followed her voice, and his heart landed solidly on her beautiful, angelic face. No wind could have carried him quickly enough to her side.

She rushed to him. "Oh, Nico. I am so sorry! We were delayed by a broken axle in Ribera and lost precious time getting the wagon repaired. I was so afraid we would miss you. It seems we arrived just in time."

At the sight of Sofia's face, Nico's heart melted like butter under a hot sun. He put down his bag and drew her into his arms, taking in the sweet fragrance of jasmine that emanated from her and stimulated his senses. Holding her close to his heart was worth the price he'd had to pay in leaving his family far behind.

He held her close, her heart beating against his in perfect harmony. They were meant for each other. How good God was to have brought them together!

Sofia's parents stood behind her, waiting their turn to greet him. Gently releasing their daughter, he turned toward Teresa and Sergio and embraced them warmly.

"Welcome home, Nico!" Teresa's words touched him with their kindness.

Less demonstrative than Teresa, Sergio placed his left hand on Nico's shoulder and heartily shook his hand with his right. "It is good to see you again, Nico. I trust you had a pleasant voyage."

"It was a good voyage as far as ocean voyages go." Now was not the time to recount to Sergio how difficult an ocean voyage was for those of lesser means or no means at all. How uncomfortable it was to travel in steerage class.

How threatening to one's physical and emotional well-being.

It was then Nico noticed Don Franco standing a short distance behind Sergio. Nico's heart leapt. "Papa!"

Nico moved toward Franco and gave him a warm hug. "Thank you for coming to meet me. I was very much looking forward to seeing you again."

"I wouldn't have missed your arrival for anything." His voice caught. "It is good to see you, my son." Franco returned Nico's warm embrace and then nodded toward Teresa. "When

Teresa learned that I had moved back to Pisano, she invited me to travel with her and her family to greet you. So, here I am." Franco's grin stretched from one ear to the other.

Nico's heart overflowed. His arrival proved to be more wonderful than he'd expected. Sofia had come. His future in-laws had come. His father had come.

The only thing missing from making his return to Sicily perfect was that Mama, Luca, Valeria, and Anna had not returned with him and could not share this precious moment of reunion.

But they would join him in just a few short months for the wedding.

Yes, the wedding.

It would take place in early September, during the grape harvest.

The time of year in which the laborers' hard work of cultivation would yield its fruit.

The time of year in which the hopes and dreams of the planting would be fulfilled.

The time of year in which his love for Sofia and hers for him would reach fruition in their holy and sacred union as husband and wife.

Chapter Twenty-One

Maria, Luca, and the girls arrived in Sicily a week before Nico and Sofia's wedding. Upon setting foot once again on her native soil, Maria was filled with joy. But upon reaching *Bella Terra*, the joy turned into sorrow when she noticed the "For Sale" sign that stood in front of the property. Although she knew her sisters had listed the estate, seeing the sign made their decision to sell more real and final. Barring a miracle, *Bella Terra* would soon be transferred to a new owner.

The night of their arrival, Maria sat with her sisters around the kitchen table, recognizing that soon *Bella Terra* would slip out of her family's hands forever. Her heart ached. "Has there been any interest in the property?"

Cristina nodded, holding on her lap her infant son Samuele, named after his maternal grandfather. "There have been a few inquiries, but nothing has materialized."

How Maria wished there were a way to keep the farm in the family! But with Luca's refusal to move back to Sicily, that option was no longer viable. Any hope she'd had of passing the land on to Nico was a lost hope, because Nico was not a legitimate son and, therefore, not eligible to inherit property. As for Valeria and Anna, by the time they grew up, it would be too late, even if they did earn enough money to purchase the farm. But would they even want to?

"There has to be a way for us to keep the farm."

"It's all for the best, Maria." Luciana's words rang hollow to Maria's ears. How could selling *Bella Terra* ever be for the best?

Just then Nico, Pietro, and Luca entered the kitchen. "So,

is there anything for us famished men to eat?"

Cristina laughed. "Yes. Right in there." She pointed to the icebox that stood to the right of the oven. "You'll find some provolone cheese in there. The bread is in the cupboard above the sink."

"I see that Sicilian women have become emancipated since we left eight years ago," Luca joked. "At one time, every woman in the kitchen would get up to cook us a meal."

"Ah, those days have passed, my dear brother-in-law." Cristina shifted the baby on her lap. "Italian women are catching up with American women."

Pietro laughed. "Or regressing, as the case may be."

Cristina chided her husband. "It's about time women realize they are equal to men in value, although different in function. Even Jesus taught as much."

"Well, I certainly won't argue with Jesus," Pietro retorted with a chuckle. He opened the icebox and withdrew a large chunk of provolone cheese. He then opened the cupboard above the sink and removed a freshly baked loaf of homemade bread. "I will serve all of you. How's that for imitating Jesus and elevating women?"

Everyone laughed.

The men joined Maria and her sisters at the table. "So, what have you wonderful ladies been discussing?" Luca asked.

Luciana spoke first. "The sale of *Bella Terra*."

Maria shot a glance at Luca. Would he reconsider at this last hour the possibility of moving back to save the farm?

Luca broke a piece of bread from the loaf. "A controversial topic, I understand."

"Well, no longer." Pietro cut a slice of the provolone cheese and handed it to Luca. "Selling is the only option left to us, given the fact that, financially, we can no longer maintain the farm."

Nico took a piece of cheese from his uncle's proffered

hand. "I wish there were some way I could buy the farm."

Maria's heart swelled at her son's words. He loved *Bella Terra* as much as she did. If he had the opportunity to purchase the farm, he would restore it to its former grandeur—and beyond. She had no doubt about that. Yet, although Nico had the heart, he lacked the money.

Luciana broke in. "Don't worry. The matter is in God's hands. We have done everything possible to keep the farm. It seems clear that God has other plans. At least, our family can be thankful to have had the opportunity to enjoy *Bella Terra* for four generations. Not many families can make that claim to their homestead."

"Let's move on to a happier topic—Nico's wedding." Luca's change of subject did not bode well for Maria. It confirmed he was adamant in his decision to remain in America, and nothing would change that decision.

"Yes!" Cristina agreed. "After Mama's death, our family needs a happy event. Samuele's birth was certainly one. Now, your wedding, Nico, will be another." Cristina smiled at her nephew. "Fill us in on what is happening with the preparations."

"Well, Sofia told me just today that her parents have planned an extravagant wedding reception. They are eager to have both sides of the family meet each other. "It will be lovely!" Luciana was all smiles.

Maria cringed. Her dreaded interaction with Teresa and her family was already beginning. And, with the union of their two children, it would only continue throughout the rest of her life. Her muscles tensed.

Cristina concurred with Luciana. "Yes, it will be lovely. Where will the reception be held?"

"In the main hall of the Grand Hotel in Ribera."

"Oh!" Pietro exclaimed. "A beautiful place! How generous of your future father-in-law!"

A twinge of envy infiltrated Maria's heart. Teresa had remained in Sicily, married a Sicilian, and was financially well-off. She herself, instead, had married Luca, gone to America to improve their financial lot, and fallen into a poverty worse than she'd experienced in Sicily. Life was not fair.

"Yes, my future father-in-law is a very kind and generous man. I am blessed to be marrying into such a wonderful family."

Maria excused herself. "It's getting late, and I'm tired after the long ocean voyage. I think I'll go to bed to rest up for the events of the coming week."

What she did not tell them is that she found the entire set of circumstances surrounding *Bella Terra*, Nico, and Teresa's family unbearable.

* * * *

The ancient bells of Pisano's Church of the Virgin rang wildly on the early September morning of Nico and Sofia's wedding day. The sky—a canopy of cloudless blue— served as a fitting backdrop for a brilliant, blazing sun and crowned the old church in which Maria and Luca had been married almost fourteen years before. In front of the church, a gushing column of water soared heavenward from the ornate circular fountain and then splashed back down into the pool of glistening water.

A soft, whispering breeze blew gently through the large, open windows of the medieval church. In front of the majestic altar, lovely arrangements of white lilies and gardenias filled the air with their sweet, intoxicating fragrance.

Maria sat in the front pew, with Valeria to her right and Anna to her left, awaiting the start of the ceremony. Luca, serving as best man, stood proudly to the side of the altar.

Maria's heart wavered between joy and sadness. Joy that Nico was happy. Sadness that she would be leaving him soon.

The church had filled with dozens of friends and relatives.

Luciana, Cristina, and Pietro sat in the pew behind Maria, Pietro holding Samuele on his lap. Don Franco and Rosa sat next to them. In the pew behind then, Salvatore and Roberto sat with their families.

Maria breathed a prayer of gratitude. God had brought her a long way in the past twenty years. He had made a way for her where there seemed to be no way.

And now, her beloved Nico, the innocent fruit of the worst trial of her life, stood in front of the altar, smiling with eagerness to greet the woman who would soon become his bride.

For those who love God all things work together for good, for those who are called according to his purpose. The Lord's words filled her with gratitude yet raised a question. Was it God's purpose for her and Luca to remain in Brooklyn?

At the sound of the organ, the congregation rose. All eyes turned toward Sofia, whose lovely, dark, almond-shaped eyes were focused only on Nico.

Valeria nudged Maria's arm. "Mama, look! Sofia has started walking down the aisle!" Valeria's excitement was that of a fourteen-year-old attending her first wedding ceremony.

Anna pressed closer, better to see the bride. "Mama, when I grow up and get married, I want a wedding gown just like Sofia's!" Anna whispered.

Maria grew pensive. One day, Luca would give Valeria and Anna into the hands of their husbands. The cycle of life repeated itself, one generation after the next.

Escorted by her father, Sofia looked magnificent, her white satin gown embroidered with lace and pearls. Her long, dark hair, piled atop her head in dozens of curls, was covered with a delicate lace veil that fell gently to her shoulders. In her hands she carried a bouquet of white roses.

Maria's heart stirred. Her little Nico—now a man—was about to be married. Where had the time gone? Yesterday, she'd held him by the hand on his first day of school. Today she would release his hand to the hand of his wife.

A pang of regret struck her full force beneath the ribs. Regret that she could not remain in Sicily to be near Nico. To enjoy his future children.

To save *Bella Terra*.

A lump formed in her throat. In a few short days, she would have to return to Brooklyn to live far away from her beloved son in a country she'd not grown to love, despite her best efforts. Luca would not bend in his decision to remain in Brooklyn, and so, as a loving wife, she would return with him, trusting that God was leading Luca in his decision for their lives.

Maria turned her attention to the bride, the young woman who, in a few moments, would become a daughter to her. Maria determined to love her as best she could.

Looking radiant, Sofia reached the altar. Her father carefully lifted her veil, tearfully planted a kiss on her cheek, and then placed his daughter's hand in Nico's. The two of them turned toward Don Vincenzo, who would officiate the ceremony.

Nico's eyes shone with love for the woman whom he'd chosen to marry and with whom he would spend the rest of his life.

And Maria's heart ached for the son she'd soon be leaving behind, perhaps forever.

Chapter Twenty-Two

The main ballroom of the Grand Hotel buzzed with excitement soon after Nico and Sofia's wedding ceremony. Large round tables were set in the finest linens, with sparkling crystal wine and water goblets placed at the head of some of the finest China Maria had ever seen. Genuine silver knives, forks, and spoons elegantly framed each plate, surrounding it like a luxurious frame.

At the center of each table, a crystal Murano vase held a long-stemmed white gardenia whose intoxicating fragrance filled the air. Elegant, floor-length coverings on the chairs added a touch of royalty to the entire room. Overhead, opulent candelabrae held lit candles that lent a festive atmosphere to the room. At the far corner of the room, a small orchestra quietly played soft classical melodies.

Clearly, Sofia's parents had done more than justice to their only daughter's wedding.

As Maria stood next to Luca at the head table with Anna and Valeria, Teresa approached her, a big smile on her beautiful face. She wore a long, shimmering sapphire-blue gown that accentuated her natural coloring. Her auburn hair was dressed in a flurry of curls atop her head. She had never looked better.

Nor happier.

"Oh, Maria, you look lovely!" Teresa kissed Maria on both cheeks and then turned to Luca. Taking both his hands in hers, she kissed him on both cheeks as well.

Finally, Teresa turned to Valeria and Anna. "How beautiful you look today!" She embraced each one. "I am so excited to welcome you into our family!"

Anna and Valeria giggled with delight.

Maria smiled, forcing herself to relax. Perhaps she was imagining false things about Teresa. Perhaps Maria's perception of Nico's mother-in-law was faulty.

Perhaps Maria had been wrong about Teresa all along.

Maria smiled. "Thank you very much, Teresa!"

The dinner bell sounded.

The orchestra stopped playing, and Sergio took his place at the front of the room. "I wish to welcome all of you to this grand celebration of Nico and Sofia's wedding. Your presence here today will mark an auspicious beginning to their lives together. And now, I would like to offer a blessing over our meal."

After his prayer, Sergio spoke again. "Before we partake of our meal, I would like to make a special announcement." He walked over to Nico and Sofia seated at the center of the head table and spoke. "Because God has graciously blessed my jewelry business throughout the world, we can now bless you. Sofia's mother and I thought long and hard about a meaningful and lasting wedding gift to give you. This is what we believe God would have for you." From his jacket pocket, Sergio withdrew a long, white envelope and handed it to Nico. "May it bless you."

All eyes were on Nico as, with trembling hands, he opened the envelope and withdrew a folded paper. Carefully, he unfolded the paper and read. His eyes grew wide with amazement and then filled with tears. He stood.

Every eye was on him in a room in which one could now hear only the soft, shallow breathing of his neighbor.

Nico turned to his father-in-law, tears streaming down his face. "There is no way I could ever thank you for this great gift." His voiced hitched.

He lifted the paper toward the guests. "As a wedding gift, my father-in-law and mother-in-law have presented Sofia and

202

me with the deed to *Bella Terra*, the farm that has been up for sale after having been in my family's possession for four generations."

Maria gasped as she grabbed and squeezed Luca's hand.

His eyes glistened.

This could not be happening! She must be dreaming!

She turned to Cristina and Luciana, who were grinning from ear to ear. "Why didn't you tell me?"

Cristina smiled. "We were sworn to secrecy so it would be a surprise for you and Nico."

The roomful of guests rose and burst into loud applause. Nico and Sofia embraced Sergio and Teresa.

Trembling, Maria sat speechless as Nico approached her with Sofia at his side. "Mama, look!"

Maria stared at the paper Nico held. It was the deed to *Bella Terra*, with his and Sofia's names listed as the new owners.

Maria burst into tears. By the grace of God, her dream had come true. God had performed a miracle. Once again, He had saved *Bella Terra* for her family.

Maria rose from her place and embraced Nico and Sofia. She then made her way toward Teresa and Sergio. "How can I ever thank both of you?"

Teresa looked at Maria with tears in her eyes. "Maria, there is no need to thank us. It is our small way to make amends to you for the great suffering you unjustly endured years ago. I am ashamed to say that I, like many others in Pisano, doubted your innocence. But the Lord watched over you and protected you from vicious tongues. So, thank Him for this gift. It is entirely His doing."

The two women warmly embraced.

Her heart full, Maria returned to her seat as the celebration began. At the end of the day, the very woman whom she'd feared the most had turned out to be the woman to whom she would be most grateful for the rest of her life.

* * * *

It was dark when Maria, Luca, Valeria, and Anna returned to *Bella Terra* after the wedding reception. The day had been long but beautiful, filled with a wide gamut of emotions. Leaning her head on Luca's shoulder, Maria reviewed the events of the day, especially the miraculous moment when Sergio presented *Bella Terra* to Nico and Sofia as a wedding gift. Never would she forget that moment. God had come through for her—and in a way she could never have imagined. Not only had the gift enabled Nico to bypass the legal sting of illegitimacy preventing inheritance, but it had also kept the farm in the family under her son's loving care. Only God could have accomplished such an amazing feat. She gave thanks in her heart for the Lord's goodness.

As the horse and wagon pulled up to the house, Maria rejoiced yet again at God's goodness. The "For Sale" sign had been removed. The house now belonged to Nico and Sofia and to their future children. They would enjoy it for the rest of their lives.

But she would not.

The wagon came to a full stop. Luca helped Maria descend and then carried a sleeping ten-year-old Anna into the house. Maria and Valeria followed him inside.

Cristina, Pietro, and Luciana had arrived shortly before them and sat at the kitchen table, drinking espresso. Samuele was upstairs, fast asleep in his crib. Pippo was curled up in a corner of the kitchen.

Maria bid Valeria goodnight and joined her sisters and brother-in-law, while Luca carried Anna up to her bed.

"You were right after all, Maria." Her sister Luciana smiled as Maria sat down at the table with them. "All things are possible when one believes."

Maria nodded. "Yes. But I must confess that when you wrote me that you and Cristina had put *Bella Terra* up for sale, my faith wavered a bit." Maria smiled. "God is so merciful! To say I was stunned by the outcome would be an understatement."

Luciana placed her hand on Maria's. "Now you can return to America in peace."

Maria's heart sank. Yes, she was now in peace about the family farm, but not about leaving her son. Tears filled her eyes. "Who knows when I will see Nico and all of you again? Because of cost, many immigrants in America die without ever seeing their families again."

Luciana rubbed the top of her sister's hand but remained silent.

"It's a difficult thing to leave one's homeland for a new world. Especially when there is little prospect of reunion."

"But, Maria," Pietro began. "I read in the newspaper about two brothers in your country who recently invented a flying machine called the 'airplane' that will one day make it possible to travel from New York to Sicily in only a matter of hours. It will be like a seagull in the sky."

Cristina gasped. "Really?"

"Yes, really." Pietro smiled and continued. "So, cheer up, Maria! With the airplane, we will be able to visit often back and forth with as much ease as traveling in a horse and wagon."

Everyone laughed.

Just then Luca returned. "What is so funny?" He pulled up a chair beside Maria.

Maria moved her chair to make room for Luca. "Pietro tells us that a new invention called an 'airplane' will soon be transporting people in the sky across the Atlantic Ocean in only a few hours instead of three weeks as it now takes by ship."

"Actually, I read the same thing in the Brooklyn newspaper. What an amazing way to travel!"

"Yes!" Pietro's face lit up. "Imagine flying across the ocean like a seagull."

Maria could only imagine.

But imagination always preceded reality.

Chapter Twenty-Three

The day of the family's departure arrived all too quickly. With Nico and Sofia's wedding now behind her and with the young couple's return to *Bella Terra* to build their lives on the family farm, there was nothing more for Maria to do. As she stood on the pier at Palermo awaiting instructions to board the ship, her heart felt like an onerous lump of lead.

"Mama, I will write to you often. I promise." Nico stood before her, his eyes filled with tears.

"I will write often, too." She embraced him and clung tightly to him for a long moment. "Take good care of yourself, my son." She turned to Sofia with a smile. "And of your precious wife." She gave Sofia a warm embrace.

Luca took Maria's arm. "It's time to board, dear one." After final hugs, Maria turned to follow Luca and her daughters aboard the ship. They made their way to the railing to bid a final farewell.

As Maria's gaze found Nico's, her heart tore completely in two. With tears streaming down her face, she waved to him one last time.

Perhaps it would be the last time forever.

As the ship pulled out of the harbor, she broke into heaving sobs and collapsed in anguish into Luca's arms.

Darkness settled over her soul like an endless night without moon or stars.

* * * *

Maria stood on her balcony overlooking the street in front of her tenement house. The first frost had nipped the remaining pink chrysanthemums lingering in a large pot that stood at her feet. On the street below, children laughed merrily as they played tag and hide-and-go-seek. Along the sidewalk, tired leaves fell from birch and maple trees, blanketing the earth beneath in a carpet of crimson, russet, and gold.

She drew in a deep breath of the brisk December air. Three months had elapsed since Nico's wedding. Her life had fallen back into its old routine of cooking, cleaning, and sewing, with weekly fellowship with the women at her church. Valeria and Anna had returned to school, and Luca had been promoted to foreman on his job of building railroads. A good thing. Maybe their dream of a better life was coming to pass after all. With her share of the proceeds from the sale of *Bella Terra* to Sergio and Teresa, she and Luca would now be able to move out of the tenement house and purchase a home of their own. And the best part was that *Bella Terra* would still remain in the family under the capable supervision of Nico and Sofia.

Not a day went by that she did not think of her son and daughter-in-law. By mid-summer of the following year, they would be parents to their firstborn child—Maria's first grandchild.

Nico had written that they had asked Don Franco to be godfather and Luciana to be godmother to the baby.

Letting go of Nico had been the most difficult thing Maria had ever done in her life. Yet, it had been the right thing—for both her and for him. For too long, she'd made a god of her son, and anything or anyone she placed above God was in violation of His first commandment.

Luca had been right. Their dream lay in America. And giving up her son had been part of fulfilling that dream. Of obeying God's call. Just last Sunday, her pastor had announced the church's decision to reopen the Brooklyn Mission. Her heart had leapt, especially at his request that she serve as director of the food program. Yes, there was a place for her in

America. A place designed specifically by God and for which He had equipped her.

She whispered a prayer of thanks.

As he'd promised, Nico wrote to her frequently, filling her in on the latest news about the family and about *Bella Terra*. In his latest letter, he'd included a message from Pietro: "Remind Maria to keep looking up. Soon she will see the seagull in the sky that will one day bring her to Sicily on its wings!"

Maria smiled. Perhaps one day she would, indeed, travel to Sicily in the sky instead of on the water. But for now, she would be content living out the purpose for which God had created her in the place where He'd placed her.

And, yes. She would keep looking up. But not for the seagull in the sky. She would keep looking up for the Son of God, Who one day would return to take His Bride to Heaven. In that perfect place, there would be no separation from loved ones. No longing for sons and grandchildren living far away.

No heart-rending conflict between two worlds.

There would be only Jesus. Only His Kingdom.

And only His peace and joy forevermore!

THE END

The Madonna of Pisano
Book One in
The Italian Chronicles Series

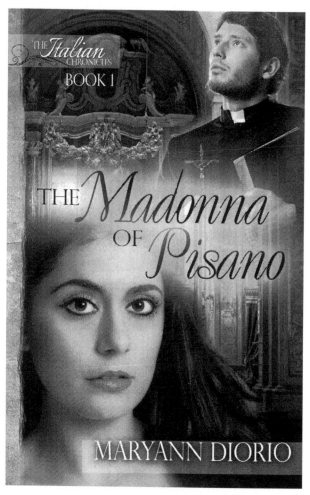

A young woman, a priest, and a secret that keeps them bitterly bound to each other…

A Sicilian Farewell
Book Two in
The Italian Chronicles Series

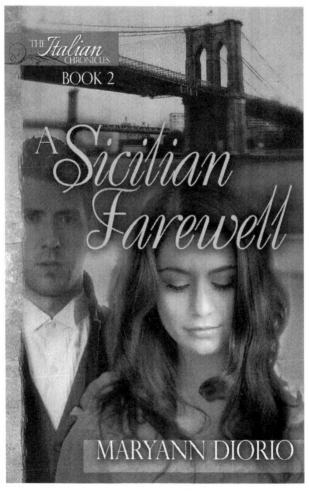

*A young man, a new land, and a dream that threatens to destroy
him, his marriage, and his mission...*

AUTHOR'S NOTE

The seed for this story was planted more than one hundred years ago, when my paternal grandfather set sail for America. The outbreak of World War I shortly after his arrival prevented my grandmother and their two children from joining him as originally planned. Seven long, grueling years later, my grandparents were reunited.

This story was written as a tribute to them—and to all immigrants—who have endured the hardships of leaving their homelands, of suffering deplorable conditions at sea, and of adapting to a New World that was often hostile and prejudiced against them.

More than that, however, this is the story of Christ's redemptive love and enduring faithfulness in the midst of the worst situations.

Because this book is a novel, much of the information has been modified to accommodate the story. Names have been altered, and circumstances and locations have been fictionalized. But its essential message remains the same: *Anyone who wants to be Christ's disciple must follow Him.*

QUESTIONS FOR GROUP DISCUSSION

NOTE: These questions may be used in a variety of ways, including book-club or reading-group discussions, in Bible-study groups dealing with the topic of fear, control, parent-child relationships, and for personal meditation.

1. Maria struggled with letting go of Nico. Because of his inauspicious beginnings, she felt she had to assume the role of protector of his life. While a mother must certainly protect her children, she is powerless to protect them from all harm. For this reason, she must learn to entrust them to God's sovereign care. Have you struggled with letting go of your children? If so, how have you dealt with the spirit of control?

2. Maria wanted to submit to God's will, but she had trouble trusting her husband's judgment about remaining in America. Have you ever struggled with trusting the decisions of those in authority over you, be it husband, pastor, or boss? If so, why? How have you applied God's Word to your situation?

3. Forgiveness is a big issue in this book. Why is forgiveness so important not only to one's spiritual health but also to one's physical well-being? Is there someone you need to forgive? Is there someone of whom you need to ask forgiveness?

4. Nico had grown to adulthood and wanted to make his own decisions for his life. As the adult child of your parents, have you faced the challenge of a controlling parent? If so, how have you handled it? How we you obey God's Word to honor your parents while setting healthful boundaries in your relationship?

5. Don Franco finds himself in a terrible situation of his own making. Having fathered Nico, Franco now faces a lifetime without a relationship with his son. Yet, Franco has sincerely repented of his sin. Do you think he should be allowed entrance into Nico's life? What does God mean in Psalm 103: 12 when He says that He has removed our transgressions from us "as far as the east is from the west"? Does forgiveness mean we should allow those who have wronged us back into our lives?

6. Despite her major flaws, Teresa ultimately acts in a loving way toward Maria. How do Teresa's actions reveal the attitude of her heart? Why is our heart attitude more important to God than our actions?

7. Maria finally discovers that God's plans for her life are far better than her own plans. Have you ever experienced a discrepancy between your plans and God's plans for your life? When you chose your plans over God's plans for you, what happened? When you chose God's plans for you over your own plans, what happened? What did you learn from both experiences?

About the Author

Dr. MaryAnn Diorio is a widely published award-wining author of fiction for both children and adults. Her passion is to proclaim truth through fiction because only truth will set people free (John 8:32). A widely published author of non-fiction as well, MaryAnn responded to God's call a few years ago to write fiction and has since published three novels, *The Madonna of Pisano*, *A Sicilian Farewell*, and *Return to Bella Terra*, all part of *The Italian Chronicles Trilogy*. She has also published two novellas, *A Christmas Homecoming* and *Surrender to Love*. MaryAnn hopes her stories will entertain and point readers to Jesus Christ, the Truth Who alone can set them free.

MaryAnn holds a PhD in French and Comparative Literature from the University of Kansas and an MFA in Writing Popular Fiction from Seton Hill University. She lives in New Jersey with her husband Dominic, a retired physician. They are blessed with two lovely adult daughters, a wonderful son-in-law, and five rambunctious grandchildren. In her spare time, MaryAnn loves to read, paint, and make up silly songs for her grandchildren.

How to Live Forever

Eternal life is a free gift offered by God to anyone who chooses to accept it. All it takes is a sincere sorrow for your sins (contrition) and a quality decision to turn away from your sins (repentance) and begin living for God.

In John 3:3, Jesus said, "Unless a man is born again, he cannot see the Kingdom of God." What does it mean to be "born again"? Simply put, it means to be restored to fellowship with God.

Man is made up of three parts: spirit, soul, and body (I Thessalonians 5:23). Your spirit is who you really are; your soul comprises your mind, your will, and your emotions; and your body is the housing for your spirit and your soul. You could call your body your "earth suit."

When we are born into this world, we are born with a spirit that is separated from God. As a result, it is a spirit without life, because God alone is the Source of life. You may have heard this condition referred to as "original sin." Why is every human being born with a spirit separated from God? Because of the sin of Adam, our first parent.

I used to wonder why I had to suffer because of Adam's sin. After all, I complained, I wasn't even there when they ate the apple! Yet, as I began to understand spiritual matters, I began to see that I was there just as a man and woman's children, grandchildren, great-grandchildren, and so on, are in the body of the man and woman in seed form before those descendants are actually born. In other words, in my children there is already the seed for their future children. In their future children will be the seed of their future children, and so on.

Now, as a parent, I can pass on to my children only what I am and what I possess. For example, I can pass on to my children only my own genetic makeup. The same is true of my husband. I possess no other genetic makeup to pass on to them.

And the same was true with Adam. Because he disobeyed God, his fellowship with God was broken. Therefore, his spirit died because it was severed from God. As a result, he could pass on to his descendants only a dead spirit—a sinful spirit, separated from God. And Adam's children could pass on to their children only a dead, sinful spirit. And so on, all the way down to you and me.

We said earlier that your spirit is the real you—who you really are. So what does it mean when our spirit is separated from God? It means that unless we are somehow reconciled to God, we will be eternally separated from him. That is what Hell is: a place of real torment resulting from eternal separation from God.

Now God is a holy God, and He will not tolerate sin in His Presence. At the same time, He is a loving God. Indeed, He IS Love! And because He loves you so much, He wanted to restore the broken relationship between you and Himself. He wanted to restore you to that glorious position of walking and talking with Him and enjoying the fullness of His blessings.

But there was a problem. Because God is infinite, only an infinite Being could satisfy the price of man's offense against God. At the same time, because man committed the offense, there had to be Someone Who would also be able to represent man in paying this price. In other words, there had to be a Being Who was both God and man in order that the price for sin could be paid.

Since God knew there was nothing man could do on his own to pay the price for his sin, God took the initiative. In the writings of John the Apostle, we learn that "God so loved the world that He gave His only-begotten Son, that whoever believes in Him shall not perish but have eternal life" (John 3:16).

What glorious GOOD NEWS! God loved you so much that He sent His one and only Son, Jesus Christ, to take the rap for your sins. Imagine that! Would you give your son to go to the electric chair for someone else? Well, that's exactly what God did! The Cross was the electric chair of Christ's day, and God gave His own Son, Jesus Christ, to go to the Cross for you!

In dying on the Cross for you, and in rising from the dead three days later, Jesus paid the price for your sins and repaired the breach between you and God the Father. Jesus restored the broken relationship between man and God. He provided mankind with the gift of eternal life.

So what does all of this mean for you? It means that if you accept Christ's gift of eternal life, you will be "born again." In other words, God will replace your dead spirit with a spirit filled with His life. "Therefore, if anyone is in Christ, he is a new creation. Old things have passed away; behold, all things have become new" (2 Corinthians 5:17).

If I offer you a gift, it is not yours until you choose to take it. The same is true with the gift of eternal life. Until you choose to take it, it is not yours. In order for you to be born again, you must reach out and take the gift of eternal life that Jesus is offering you now. Here is how to receive it:

"Lord Jesus, I come to You now just as I am—broken, bruised, and empty inside. I've made a mess of my life, and I need You to fix it. Please forgive me of all of my sins. I accept You now as my personal Savior and as the Lord of my life. Thank You for dying for me so that I might live. As I give You my life, I trust that You will make of me all that You've created me to be. Amen."

If you prayed this prayer, please write to me to let me know. I will send you some information to help you get started in your Christian walk. Also, I encourage you to do three important things:

1) Get yourself a Bible, and begin reading it, starting with the Gospel of John.

2) Find yourself a good church that preaches the full Gospel. Ask God to lead you to a church where you can learn His righteous ways of thinking and living.

3) Set aside a time every day for prayer. Prayer is simply talking to God as you would to your best friend.

I congratulate you on making the life-changing decision to accept Jesus Christ! It is the most important decision of your life. Mark down this date because it is the date of your spiritual birthday. Be assured of my prayers for you as you grow in your Christian walk. God bless you!

Other Books by Dr. MaryAnn Diorio

A Christmas Homecoming

When Sonia Pettit's teenage daughter goes missing for seven long years, Sonia faces losing her mind, her family, and her faith.

Available on Amazon, NOOK, Kobo, and iTunes.

Surrender to Love

When young widow and life coach, Dr. Teresa Lopez Gonzalez, travels to Puerto Rico to coach the granddaughter of her mother's best friend, Teresa faces her unwillingness to surrender to God's will for her life. In the process, she learns that only by losing her life will she truly find it.

Available on Amazon, NOOK, Kobo, and iTunes.

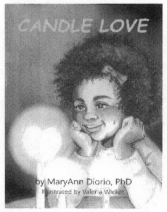

Candle Love

Four-year-old Keisha has a new baby sister. But Keisha doesn't want a new baby sister. Keisha is afraid that Mama will love Baby Tamara more than Mama loves her. But when Mama shows Keisha three special candles, Keisha learns that there is always enough love for everyone because the more one shares love, the more love grows.

Available on Amazon, NOOK, Kobo, and iTunes.

Who Is Jesus?

Introduce your child to the true Jesus of the Bible.

Available on Amazon, NOOK, Kobo, and iTunes.

226

Toby Too Small

Toby Michaels is small. Too small to be of much good to anyone. But one day, Toby discovers that it's not how big you are on the outside that matters; it's how big you are on the inside.

Available on Amazon, NOOK, Kobo, and iTunes.

Do Angels Ride Ponies?

A handicapped boy discovers the power of faith to achieve the impossible.

Available on Amazon, NOOK, Kobo, and iTunes.

SOCIAL MEDIA SITES

You will find Dr. MaryAnn on the following social media sites:|

Website: www.maryanndiorio.com
Blog (Matters of the Heart):
www.networkedblogs.com/blog/maryanndiorioblog
Amazon Author Central:
www.amazon.com/author/maryanndiorio
Authors Den: www.authorsden.com/maryanndiorio
BookBub.com: www.bookbub.com/authors/maryann-diorio
Facebook: www.facebook.com/DrMaryAnnDiorio
Twitter: http://twitter.com/@DrMaryAnnDiorio
Goodreads: www.goodreads.com/author/show/6592603
LinkedIn: www.linkedin.com/in/maryann-diorio-phd-dmin-mfa-99924513/
Pinterest: www.pinterest.com/drmaryanndiorio/
Google+: http://plus.google.com/u/0/+DrMaryAnnDiorio
Instagram: www.instagram.com/drmaryanndiorio/
Library Thing: www.librarything.com/profile/drmaryanndiorio
Vimeo: https://vimeo.com/user46487508
YouTube: www.youtube.com/user/drmaryanndiorio/
BlogTalk Radio: www.blogtalkradio.com/drmaryanndiorio

TopNotch Press
A Division of MaryAnn Diorio Books
PO Box 1185
Merchantville, NJ 08109
FAX: 856-488-0291
Email: info@maryanndiorio.com